The White Star Continuity
Book 5

FULL CIRCLE

by

Shannon Hollis

Before Daniel Burke was the "real Indiana Jones,"
Cate Wells thought he was everything she could ever
want. Then, after a humiliating experience eight years
ago, she realized she was wrong. Now Cate needs
Daniel's help, and it's clear the heat between them
hasn't dimmed. But is she sleeping with the man…
or the image?

Don't miss the final installment
of The White Star
DESTINY'S HAND
by Lori Wilde,
available June, Book 6

Blaze™

Dear Reader,

Welcome to book five of THE WHITE STAR miniseries!
I'm thrilled to be part of it, and hope you enjoy the next
installment, which features academic Cate Wells and
adventurer archaeologist Daniel Burke.

Theirs is a reunion story—an ever-popular plot. But
why is it so popular? What is it about the "do-over" that
fascinates us so? Is it the chance to revisit an old love and
see what has changed—and what has not? Or is it the
chance to remember what went wrong—and get it right
this time? Because we all know that our first love may
not be our true love. But when it is, as Cate and Daniel
discover, getting it right can cover anything from that
first magical kiss…to…well, let's find out!

To find out more about THE WHITE STAR miniseries,
surf to eHarlequin.com or visit me on the Web at
www.shannonhollis.com.

Warmly,

Shannon Hollis

Books by Shannon Hollis

HARLEQUIN BLAZE

HARLEQUIN TEMPTATION

FULL CIRCLE

Shannon Hollis

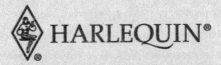

HARLEQUIN®

TORONTO • NEW YORK • LONDON
AMSTERDAM • PARIS • SYDNEY • HAMBURG
STOCKHOLM • ATHENS • TOKYO • MILAN • MADRID
PRAGUE • WARSAW • BUDAPEST • AUCKLAND

For my fellow writers in the San Francisco Area and
Vancouver Island chapters of Romance Writers of America.

Acknowledgments

Thanks to Carrie Alexander, Kristin Hardy, Jeanie London
and Lori Wilde—true professionals and a pleasure
to work with. Thanks also to Dr. David Andersen,
paleogeologist, who knew exactly
where I could find a plesiosaur.

ISBN 0-373-79258-1

FULL CIRCLE

FOR TRUE LOVE WOULD ENDURE...

Princess Batu stood on the dais of the Hall of a Thousand Pillars, two steps below her sister, Queen Anan, and the queen's husband of one moon, the brave soldier Egmath.

Batu's heart broke afresh at the sight of him—his thighs and arms with the strength of cedars and his eyes with the gentleness of a dove. Across the distance that separated them and behind the straight, commanding figure of the queen, their gazes met, warm with the love that must forever be unacknowledged. Batu thanked the gods that they had not denied her the gift of seeing his face one last time—for the news that the queen was to announce was not good.

"People of the kingdom," Anan said in tones that carried both hope and authority, "join with me in prayer that our army will be victorious. The Pharaoh of Egypt covets our lands and prosperity, and even now his forces advance upon us like jackals upon a herd of gazelles. In vain have we negotiated treaty. In vain have we sent tribute. Ramses demands utter capitulation, but this I will not do. Today our army marches. Today the gods will send victory!"

A roar of cheering erupted in the great hall, and soon a chant arose: "Egmath! Egmath!"

Head high, his hand on his sword, Egmath strode forward without a backward glance, and the soldiers lining the dais fell in behind him. Anan retired to her rooms at the palace, to spend the rest of the day on her knees before the altars of the gods entreating their favor.

Batu retired to her own room, but she could not pray or light the scented oils of sacrifice. All she could do was stand at the window, which looked to the south from whence the Egyptian army would come, and think of Egmath. He would be attending to the arming of his troops now. Each man would strap on his leather and bronze armor, and put a bridle gleaming with oil and gold trim over his horse's head. Each man would look to sword and shield, brave with the device of the lion, symbol of the royal house.

Trumpets sounded, and the army marched in all its splendor through the gates of the city, past the river where only one full moon ago, she and Egmath had lain on the banks and she had experienced the ecstasy that is the crown of love. In the days since, she held that memory close to her heart, taking it out to turn it over and marvel at it only when she was alone in the dark of night. She kept it as close to her heart as Egmath kept her ivory star amulet to his.

She had a memory. He had the White Star.

It was enough.

Batu watched at her window for seven days and seven nights. With the coming of the red dawn, a single messenger, bloodied and beaten, staggered through the gates and, with the last reserves of his strength, collapsed in the Hall of a Thousand Pillars.

Batu left her window and raced into the hall. Forgetting her dignity as queen, Anan ran down the steps of the dais, her robes billowing around her, and both sisters fell to their knees beside the messenger.

"Soldier, what news?" cried Anan, while Batu cradled the man's head on her lap. Blood from a scalp wound—a sword? a spear?—smeared the white linen of her shift.

The palace physician hurried toward them, but even Batu could see that the messenger had already begun his journey to the halls of the gods.

"It was—a rout, Lady," he gasped. "The armies of Egypt are as locusts on the ground. The kingdom must fall. None are left to defend it."

"What of Egmath?" Batu could barely pronounce the words, so frozen with fear was she.

"Fallen, my lady." The messenger's voice was fading as he looked to Anan. "As I fled toward the city I saw the royal standard engulfed by the enemy. Egmath sent me. He bids you and the princess to flee. Take only a change of clothing and some food."

"Sent he no other message?" cried Batu. Oh, could she not go onto the field of battle and find him herself? Was there no hope that he might still live?

"He—he sends to the queen..."

"Yes?" Anan clutched his garment.

"...that his love is as a white star in the heavens, that it will never die...."

The messenger's spirit completed its journey to the gods and his body slumped in Batu's arms. She knelt, her own heart dying in her chest, as she realized that

Egmath's last message had been to her, and her alone. But that strength, that gentle humor, that bravery born of love...all were lost to her forever.

Anan sat on the floor, as pale as her own shift, her eyes blank with terror. "They will make slaves of us, Batu," she whispered. "I shall be the Pharaoh's concubine at best, if the gods smile upon me."

"You will not." Batu laid the messenger's body on the glossy stone floor with care, then pulled her sister's unresisting form to her feet. "Egmath's last thoughts were of us. We will not betray him by allowing ourselves to be captured and taken to Egypt in chains."

Before the sun had fallen another finger's breadth toward the horizon, the princess without a lover and the queen without a kingdom had stolen out of the palace even as the conquering army marched in triumph through the gates of the city. Batu carried only two linen shifts, some dried figs, dried meat and a skin of water. She would never see her home again—but that did not matter now. All that mattered was that Egmath's last thoughts had been of her—and that meant more to her than all the jewels Anan carried wrapped in a linen towel.

As the sun fell and the wings of the goddess of night enfolded the desert, two slender figures stole over the cliffs behind the city and vanished among the dunes, to be seen again no more....

TO BE CONTINUED....

1

THERE WAS NO SUCH THING as a dead man's curse.

In the murky twilight of two hundred feet of silty water, Daniel Burke felt like arguing the point as he squinted through his mask, searching for the ribs of the sixteenth-century Basque galleon on the ocean floor.

This recovery expedition had been cursed with everything from bad organization to shoddy safety practices, and the fact that Daniel knew he was only here to give it some legitimacy with the inevitable press orgy didn't help. He should have said no when the Society for the Preservation of Antiquities had approached him. He should have told them that water wasn't his element—he belonged in the desert, where layers of sandstone and petrified ash yielded their secrets as reluctantly as a beautiful woman, where caves and hills whispered to him of long-lost civilizations.

But no. The Society had promised him enough money to fund his next trip to Asia Minor, and he, like any dope, had fallen for it.

If the Society's information was correct, the master of the whaling ship had been the first European to set foot on the shores of the New World. Not Columbus.

Not Cabot or Cartier. But a wily Basque captain who had seen the money that could be made out of whale oil from the dangerous waters off the Atlantic coast of Canada. Daniel had no idea how many trips the ship had made before those waters had claimed her, but the success of this expedition and maybe even his own reputation were waiting on the results.

Not to mention the kid's father.

The reason he was down here on an emergency rescue mission.

Ian MacPherson was a nineteen-year-old archaeology student swabbing decks in exchange for the SPA's exclusive right from the Canadian government to study the site. The fact that the kid's father was a high-ranking Canadian cabinet minister was the reason the Society had its permit—and Ian. The dumb-ass had swiped some diving equipment and gone over the side alone this morning, and some fifteen minutes had passed before anyone had noticed. Daniel was going to haul him back aboard by the scruff of his neck and ship him back to his father on the chopper.

As soon as he found him.

"I got not'ing forty feet from the site." The transmitter in Daniel's ear clicked as Luc Pinchot reported in from his left.

"Moi non plus," said the diver on his right.

"Another ten feet," Daniel said. "He has to have gone in to look at the site. He'll be here somewhere."

"The currents 'ere are pretty mean," Luc said. "''E could have been swep' to de nort'."

"One can only hope." Daniel's voice was grim. The

little weasel was going to wish he'd been washed up on the Newfoundland rocks after Daniel got through with him. The untimely death of the cabinet minister's son was not the kind of publicity he needed right now.

A freak current cleared the silt for a split second— just long enough for him to see a flash of yellow neoprene in the beam of his lamp. "Straight ahead, twenty feet," he snapped. "Looks like our boy got himself into trouble."

The three divers put a little steam on and silt boiled around them as they surrounded Ian the Idiot. Somehow he'd managed to get his right foot caught between two heavy timbers—and was held down like a ferret in a leg trap.

"AND THEN WHAT HAPPENED?"

Jah-Redd Jones, former NBA basketball star, Oscar nominee, and now the latest king of the talk-show hosts, leaned forward and his studio audience took a collective breath in anticipation.

Daniel brushed at his jeans and work boots and gave a modest smile that hid the disgust that hadn't quite faded, four months later.

"We worked his foot loose and got him up to the surface. But not before we discovered that the galleon had been used for more than just transporting whale oil." He grinned at the camera, drawing out the suspense, milking the extra second for all it was worth. "I figure the captain was an opportunistic kind of guy—because when an English ship blundered across its path, probably blown off course by a storm, he took the opportunity to relieve it of some of its cargo. Which in this case happened to be cases of Flemish wine and about fifty gold guineas."

The audience gasped and even Jah-Redd, pro that he was, sat back on the interviewer's couch with a big goofy grin. "Daniel Burke, man, there's a reason they call you 'the real Indiana Jones.' Folks, can't you see this as a movie? Huh?"

The studio audience burst into applause, the women in the front row whistling and stamping as if Daniel were an exotic dancer and they wanted to tuck bills in his G-string.

Daniel masked a sigh and held the grin between his teeth. His reputation was what brought in the funding. The fact that it was more of a media creation than reality didn't make it any less useful. Besides, there was a curvy woman in the front row and he'd bet a hundred bucks she'd be waiting at the street door when he left after his segment. While the audience clapped, he toyed with a few interesting possibilities.

"So tell me," Jah-Redd said, leaning on his elbows and clasping his hands under his chin, "is it true that the Canadian government gave you the Order of Canada for saving Ian MacPherson's life?"

"No." Daniel brought his wandering thoughts back to business. "There was talk, but it's hard to take a medal for doing what you'd do for any member of your crew." *And saving a kid from his own stupidity isn't worth a medal.* "The divers with me helped get him free, and that's when we discovered the gold. It was in a strong-box directly under where Ian was trapped. His struggles to get free had disturbed the silt that covered it."

Jah-Redd appealed to the audience. "Save a person's life, find a buried treasure, all in a day's work. How many people would like a job like that?" The audience applauded again.

"I'd like a man like that!" hollered the curvy woman, and Daniel mentally awarded himself a hundred bucks.

"Not married, huh?" Jah-Redd cocked a knowing eyebrow in Daniel's direction. "Girlfriend, significant other, rows of willing concubines?"

Daniel had a flash of memory—a wide and sensuous mouth, long-lashed eyes, sun-streaked brown hair spread on red sandstone—and covered the mental lapse with a laugh.

"None of the above. Not too many women will tolerate a pot hunter, even when we clean up nice. We spend half the year in remote locations and the other half holed up in dark offices writing research papers about them. Not the best conditions to nurture a relationship, I'm afraid."

"By *pot hunter* I take it you don't mean the green leafy stuff." The audience laughed along with its host. "How did you get started, er, pot hunting?"

"Did you ever dig holes in the backyard as a kid, hoping to get to Australia?"

Jones nodded. "Now I just take Qantas and let them do all the work."

Daniel smiled while the audience cracked up. "Well, I just never stopped digging. After my folks were killed when I was six, I went to live with my godparents. I found a Native American artifact in their yard in the burbs when I was twelve, and I knew then I wanted to be an archaeologist. So I went to the University of Chicago, then did postgrad work at the University of New Mexico, specializing in the work of a particular Anasazi potter. From there I assisted in a couple of Central American digs, and that of course led to Argentina and—"

"The Temecula Treasure."

"Right."

On the screen above them, a clip began to play from the documentary PBS had done last year on his discovery of a trove of gold artifacts. Audience members who hadn't seen it yet gasped. He couldn't blame them. He'd done the same when he'd realized that, instead of finding pottery, he'd stumbled on a grave belonging to a much later civilization—one that believed the dead needed jewelry in the afterlife. Spectacular jewelry.

"Did you get to keep any of it?" Jah-Redd wanted to know.

Daniel shook his head. "It belongs to the Argentinian government, of course. We had six months to study it all before our permit expired and we turned everything over."

But not before he'd published the second of two groundbreaking papers that had made his name in the academic world and clinched the funding that made his projects possible.

Beautiful funding. Nonacademic funding that took him all over the world and satisfied his itch to get his fingers into every stratum of soil this planet had to offer. That was his real passion. Discovery. It was the media that had latched on to a couple of lucky finds and branded him with this adventurer persona. After the *Newsweek* article, someone had even sent him a fedora and a leather whip, which had sent the archaeology department's assistant into gales of laughter and made him the butt of half disgusted, half admiring jokes for months afterward. The other faculty members might gripe in private about his celebrity, but no one complained when it was grant-writing time and the money poured in.

Jah-Redd had returned to the subject of women, prompted, no doubt, by the screaming in the front row. "It's hard to believe that a man like you—you're what, twenty-eight? Thirty?—wouldn't have someone important in his life, though," his host said with mock gravity. On the screen, still shots of three actresses appeared. "Indiana Jones loved three women over the years of the movies. Which one would be most like your ideal? The tomboy adventurer with the broken heart, the blond bombshell or the seductress?"

Daniel laughed while the audience waited, the expectant silence punctuated by blatant come-ons and even a boob flash—mercifully unseen by the studio cameras—from the front row.

Again, her face drifted through his mind's eye, laughing down at him from some impossible rock outcropping while she trusted her life to bits of metal jammed in where metal was never meant to go.

"I'd have to say my ideal woman would have the brains and adventurous spirit of Marion Ravenwood, the loyalty of Short Round, and the sexual curiosity of Dr. Elsa Schneider. But of course, a woman like that already exists—I believe you snapped her up for yourself, Jah-Redd."

The audience laughed and applauded, and while

Jones announced they were cutting to commercial, Daniel sat motionless while memory attacked him.

Because a woman like that did exist.

And he'd chased her out of his life long ago.

2

"SEXUAL CURIOSITY, my aunt Fanny!"

Cate Wells snapped off the TV with a vicious stab of her thumb and threw the remote—not against the wall, because that would damage it—but into the corner of the couch, where it bounced off a pillow and onto the floor.

Fuming, she rammed her feet into slippers shaped like the man-eating bunny from *Monty Python and the Holy Grail* and stalked into her bedroom. The nerve of that man! He was everywhere she looked these days— on *The Jah-Redd Jones Show,* in the papers, even in the Vandenberg University bookstore, where the obnoxious book he was so enthusiastically promoting on talk shows was stacked ten deep on a front-table display.

As if anybody but a gullible public could mistake him for a serious scholar and field researcher when the wretched thing was called *Lost Treasures of the World: Adventures in Archaeology.*

How utterly lame.

As lame as those women in the studio audience, screaming and drooling like a lot of hormone-ridden teenagers. Most of them were old enough to be his mother. Granted, the cheekbones and the iron planes of his jaw hadn't changed in the eight years since she'd seen him last. And the obliging close-ups of the camera had shown eyes that were as dark and shuttered as they'd ever been. But the boy she'd fallen for on the short southern nights of the dig in Mexico where they'd worked together for one enchanted summer was gone forever. That boy had shared her love of discovery—whether it was the secrets hidden by layers of soil and rock, or the secrets hidden by diffidence and sexual uncertainty.

Sexual curiosity, indeed!

Thank heavens she'd never told a soul about their aborted relationship—not even her closest girlfriends or her parents in San Diego. He had been a secret she was prepared to take to her grave. What a pity he hadn't been quite so discreet.

Cate pulled the five-hundred-thread-count Egyptian cotton sheet up to her chin and willed herself to go to sleep. She had appointments in the morning and a paper to proof that was guaranteed to knock the socks off the tenure committee, and she needed a clear head.

But the sight of Daniel, older but just as charismatic and sexy in his jeans and boots, disturbed her dreams as thoroughly as he'd disturbed her peace of mind—and, it must be confessed, her body. Her brain, usually so dependable, decided to take her on a trip down memory lane. The dig site, baking under the relentless Mexican sun, where archaeology students from universities across the country had been cycled in and out for brute labor disguised as summer credit. A moon the size of a gold doubloon lighting Daniel's face as he'd leaned in, as dirty and sweaty as she was, for that first kiss. That last night, when they'd slipped off to find a cool cave to lay their sleeping bags in, where she'd panicked at the very last moment and run, humiliating herself and no doubt earning his undying contempt.

But oh, those days between the first kiss and the cave…those days had been filled with her first experience of intense sexual longing. He had been all she'd been able to think about—her body becoming a kind of tuning fork with a single frequency: Daniel Burke. Lying here in the dark of her bedroom, her unsatisfied lust triggered dreams of him. A stealthy hand cupping her derriere as the group of students stood listening to a field lecture. A hard thigh pressing hers as they ate together in camp. Kisses that practically blew the top off her head as they abandoned the others and sneaked off behind rock outcroppings to explore each other in private.

At four in the morning, Cate woke to find herself wet and aching, staring into the dark.

She'd followed his career—it was pretty hard to avoid it, with *Newsweek* and the *American Journal of Archaeology* doing their very best to give his exploits legitimacy. It was only at moments like this, in the deepest dark, when her defenses were down and she was unable to keep the lid of professional disdain on her natural honesty, that she could admit how much it had hurt when no call or letter had ever come. It wasn't as though she was hard to find. All the faculty at Vandenberg were listed on the Web site, and she was in the Queens phone directory. When she'd made associate professor at Columbia and then taken the position at Vandenberg shortly afterward, the papers had made a nice little fuss about nabbing such a coveted job out from under hundreds of candidates when she was so young.

No, it was clear that when Daniel had told Jah-Redd about wanting someone who was loyal and who had sexual curiosity, he had been making a dig at her.

Bastard. She would absolutely not waste another thought on him. Her body could just calm down. Instead of masturbating and giving him control of her body again, she would think about her paper. That would do the trick.

She would think about her career plan, which was laid out in nice, achievable steps where she did the right things and talked with the right people, and success was a natural outgrowth of a good strategy. Columbia, to start. Then the move to Vandenberg, a private university that had its quirks but whose reputation was stellar. Tenure by the age of thirty. After that, perhaps a book of her own. A serious, scholarly work, unlike that of some people she could name.

Success. The right career path, a book, a reputation people would give their eyeteeth for. That was what was important here, not memories of the past, no matter how disturbing.

Despite big helpings of positive visualization, it was only thanks to an extra-large latte (no whip) that she was able to get herself to the gym, then to the subway and onto the campus a couple of hours later. The walk across the quad to the Horn Building normally lifted her spirits, especially on an early summer day like this, when the sun warmed the granite dome of the Memorial Library to terra-cotta and students sat on the amphitheater-like plaza steps like flocks of birds sunning themselves.

Darn Daniel anyway. He'd managed to take even that small pleasure from her.

Which wasn't the most mature and logical attitude to take, but she wasn't feeling mature or logical this morning, thank you very much.

In her tiny but carefully decorated office, Cate dumped the day's mail on her desk, put her purse in the bottom left drawer, and extracted the paper with its sticky tabs and red corrections from her briefcase. A glance at the calendar told her she had thirty minutes before her first appointment, a woman named Morgan Shaw who wanted to talk about an artifact but who would not tell Anne Walters, the department administrative assistant, a thing more.

Cate gave a mental shrug. Every now and again she got one of these—someone who dug up an arrowhead and figured they'd discovered a Native American burial site, or someone who found something in Uncle Lester's attic that had to be an ancient treasure. She'd become quite skilled at letting people down gently.

She turned her attention to the mail. Circulars, notices, memorandums from the department head, who knew better than to kill trees by sending memos in hard copy, but insisted on doing so to make himself feel he'd accomplished something. Cate sighed and picked up a glossy brochure giving her final notice of a conference in Big Sur, California.

Then a name caught her eye.

Keynote speaker and featured presenter: Daniel Burke, "the real Indiana Jones." Dr. Burke will present the keynote speech at Saturday's luncheon and will also present his latest paper, Silent Voices: Tracing the Trade Routes through Pre-Columbian Pottery, *on Friday night. After the presentation, Dr. Burke will sign his new book, an event that will be open to the public.*

"Be still my heart." Bad enough his face invaded her living room. Worse that it had inhabited her dreams. But to barge uninvited into her office, her citadel where only she was in control—that was just too much.

Cate aimed the brochure at the trash can and fired it with a flick of her wrist, where it landed with a swish amid a lot of other things that she didn't need and no longer cared about.

The digital clock on her desk flipped from 9:29 to 9:30 and Anne Walters leaned in the door. "Dr. Wells? Ms. Shaw is here for her appointment."

Cate turned her back on the trash can and its obnoxious contents. "Thanks, Anne. Send her in."

"I'm going to run out for another coffee. Want one?"

Anne knew the location of every espresso bar in a ten-block radius. "You are a goddess. Extra-large, no whip."

"Back in fifteen."

Morgan Shaw, tall, blond and professional, came in with a confident stride and a hand outstretched in greeting. When Cate shook it, she got the impression of self-assurance mixed with a whole lot of anticipation. Whatever the woman had to show her, it meant a lot to her.

Ms. Shaw shook back her mane of hair and smiled. "Dr. Wells, thank you for seeing me."

Cate waved her into the guest chair in front of her desk and settled herself in her own. "Did Anne offer you something to drink?"

"Yes, she did, thanks."

"No trouble finding us?"

"Not at all. I got very good directions from my sister, Cassandra. I'd like to thank you personally for rescuing her a few months ago."

Cate grinned with delight. Earlier in the year she had escaped the city and had been four-wheeling through the woods upstate, on her way back from her therapy cliff—the one she climbed when she really needed to clear her head and find her center again. She'd offered a lift to a couple of stranded hikers, and had stayed in touch ever since. "Cass is your sister? Then I'm doubly pleased to meet you. I understand you have an artifact that you wanted to show me," she prompted. "How did you come by it?"

Morgan leaned over and pulled her leather tote into her lap. "I have an antique shop in Fairfield, Connecticut. I found this in a late-Victorian dresser that was part of the stock I bought along with the shop." She opened a cardboard container much like the ones the post office used, and extracted a wooden box. "I was hoping you could tell me a little about it."

Cate pulled the box closer. This was no relic from Uncle Lester's attic. Weighing no more than her low-profile laptop, the box was so ornately carved that there was no room for a single extra figure on its surface. She tried to separate the images to discover some meaning or clue as to its provenance, but the figures merged into one another, almost seeming to lose themselves before she could fix them in place. There were flowers, a sun and a hawk, what looked like a tree and the wavy lines that in most cultures denoted water. There were animals—a hippo, a lion—and plants. A lotus. Reeds, maybe. There were musical instruments—a lyre, or was it a harp? A flute—or was it a reed next to a crocodile? And among the images were symbols, regular and uniform enough to indicate written language.

"This is amazing." When Morgan nodded, Cate realized she'd spoken aloud.

"I can't even tell what kind of wood it is, much less figure out what the carvings mean," Morgan said. "I thought maybe cherry? Walnut? Not ebony, because it's kind of reddish-brown."

"That much I do recognize." Cate turned the box over to examine its underside. She caught a faint whiff of some kind of spice. "If I'm not mistaken, it's bubinga, an extremely hard and durable wood from Africa. The person who carved it was obviously a very skilled craftsman."

"Can you tell how old it is?"

"Other than 'old'?" Cate, with the box at eye level, smiled over the top of it at her visitor. "I can't be sure, but at a guess I'd say more than two thousand years. From some of the cuts in the curved lines, here, I'd say they used a hand awl, which might even put it at three thousand years."

Daniel would know.

Yes, but the likelihood of Daniel seeing this box was nil, wasn't it?

She lowered the box and ran her fingers along a row of what looked like monkey heads. Or maybe they were irises. The more she looked, the harder it was to tell. "How does it open?"

Morgan lifted her shoulders in a shrug. "I was hoping you could tell me. There's a compartment inside, I know that much, because I ran it through the security check at the train station on the way here and peeked at the monitor. But I have no idea if it contains anything, or how it's opened."

Lost Treasures of the World, whispered that treacherous voice in her head. *Daniel might have some information.*

Cate stifled the voice and glanced at Morgan. "Do you mind if I take some photographs? I could show the pictures to one or two of my colleagues and they might be able to identify the culture that produced these carvings."

Morgan shook her head. "Not at all."

Cate kept her field camera in the office just for moments like these. She put in a fresh roll of high-resolution film and tore the top sheet off her desk blotter to make a clean white surface. A ruler next to the box gave perspective. Then she carefully photographed each side in close-up, at midrange and from a couple of feet away, just as she'd been taught all those years ago in Mexico.

"We can learn as much from the matrix in which a piece of pottery is embedded as we can from the potsherd itself." The voice of their supervising prof, Dr. Andersen, sounded in her memory. "Your photographs should include this information. It could be important."

Cate was surprised she remembered that much—the day they'd excavated the midden and found the fragments of pottery was the day Daniel Burke had arrived. Cate's memory of anything but him after that point had been burned away by the force of their attraction. There was a thesis for you—*The Passionate Flame: Biological Urges and the Death of Brain Cells.*

"—long it might take?"

Cate blinked and resisted the urge to roll her eyes at herself. Damn that Daniel Burke anyway. Now she looked like an airhead.

"I'm sorry, what was that?" She put the camera back in its case and ran a slow hand over the surface of the box. She was not normally given to touching things. Her colleague Julia was always doing that, though—rubbing fabric between her fingers, stroking passing dogs in Central Park. Now Cate felt the same urge to touch this box. Something about the carvings invited you to follow them with your fingers, to touch them as though they were braille and had a message for you.

"I was just wondering how long it might take to get an opinion from your colleague," Morgan said, doing a good job of disguising her eagerness. But Cate knew that feeling—that excitement when you were *this close* to finding an answer that had eluded you. Some said that curiosity killed the cat. But curiosity was an archaeologist's best friend.

"I'm not sure," Cate hedged. Out of the corner of her eye, she saw the glossy brochure advertising the conference, facedown in the trash.

Daniel might help.

No. No way. Not to satisfy her own curiosity, not to help out Ms. Morgan Shaw, would she get on a plane and fly across the country to see Daniel Burke strutting around Big Sur as though he were God's gift to archaeology and women.

"A couple of weeks? A month?" Morgan persisted.

What are you afraid of?

Nothing. The thought was ludicrous.

So he had a rep for flamboyance. So he'd been on *Jah-Redd* last night. The fact remained that he was an authority on ancient symbology, and if anyone would know about this box, it would be him. Besides, she hadn't taken in a conference since that one in D.C. last year. And she hadn't seen the ocean since the Jurassic period—or at least it seemed that way.

Think of it. Big breakers crashing on the beach. Someone else doing the cooking. Late-night conversations with experts from all over the world, in fields as diverse as geology, history and archaeology.

The beach. No walls. No taxis honking and sirens screaming. Nothing but the vast Pacific, stretching out into infinity, and seagulls telling you about it as they wheeled overhead.

"A couple of weeks," she said suddenly, handing the box back to Morgan Shaw, who tucked it carefully into its container. "I'm considering a conference next weekend. If I go, I would show these photographs to an archaeologist there."

A smile as broad and warm as the California sun broke across the other woman's face. "I'd love it if you could help. I don't know what it is about this box. It's not an obsession—it's more like an itch that I just have to scratch, you know?"

Cate did know.

Because Daniel Burke had been the itch she'd been longing to scratch for the last eight years.

3

"FEEL LIKE HAVING A DRINK with me tonight before you head home?"

There was a pause while Cate imagined Julia Covington checking her watch and raising her eyebrows. "Cate, it's ten in the morning and already you're scheduling drinks?"

"I feel the need." Thinking about a nice, cold glass of chardonnay was better than thinking about Daniel Burke. "So, can you? Or do you have plans already with Alex?"

"Just dinner, but we don't eat till late. The usual place at six?"

"I'll be there," Cate promised with a little more fervency than strictly necessary.

Jake's was a real Irish pub just down the street from the Museum of Antiquities, where Julia was a curator. You could get anything from a pint of Guinness to a good French champagne—or a California chardonnay, if that happened to be on your mind. Plus they served shrimp wontons that were about as far from Ireland as you could get, but that Cate adored.

The waiter put a big plate of them between Cate and

Julia, and Cate dipped one in rice vinegar, savoring the tartness against the sweet shrimp on her tongue.

"I've been waiting for this all day," she sighed.

"I've been waiting to find out what the emergency is." Julia sipped her cabernet and eyed her friend with that narrowed gaze that meant Cate hadn't fooled her one bit. "Either something happened at the department or you've got man trouble."

Man, she was good. "Both."

Julia leaned forward with interest. "Did they hire some hot new prof who actually has looks to go with his brains?"

"No such luck. A woman named Morgan Shaw came to see me. She has an antique store in Connecticut, and she brought an artifact with her. A wooden box. Kind of fascinating, all carved with nature figures, flowers and musical instruments. Very Egyptian looking, but not Egyptian, of course. If that were the case, I wouldn't be having such a hard time dating and placing it."

"Do you want me to have a look?" She and Julia had met at an archaeology symposium a year or two after Cate had graduated. Two women in a man's field, they had gravitated together in self-defense, then had become friends. Since she'd taken up the curatorship at the museum, Julia would consult with Cate once in a while when she ran across a particularly interesting piece. But this was different.

"No, it's not that. I want you to talk me out of going to California."

Julia sat back and stared at her. "Not getting the connection, babe."

"I don't even make sense to myself. Did you see *Jah-Redd* last night?"

"Did the Romans invade Britain? Of course I saw it. How about that Indiana Jones guy with the Clive Owen mojo? Was he hot or what?"

Cate sighed and wished she'd gone home and poured a glass of whatever was in her fridge. "That Indiana Jones guy is Daniel Burke, who, despite his truly annoying tendency to hog the media spotlight, is an expert in ancient artifacts, specializing in symbology. He's going to be at a conference in California and I'm toying with the idea of going to it and showing him some photos of the box."

"There isn't anybody closer?"

"Not with his experience."

"Don't you have classes? You can't just skip off to California, can you?"

"Reading week is next week, where theoretically the students study for exams the following week." Theoretically. She couldn't imagine any of her students actually doing it. "I assume that's why the conference is scheduled then."

"So go." Julia was looking at her with a *what's the big deal?* expression.

"I...um..."

Understanding dawned in her friend's eyes. "Oh, my God. You have a history with this guy."

Cate nodded miserably. "And not a good one, either."

"Professionally or personally?"

"Personally."

"Cate Wells, how could I not have known this? You and the 'real Indiana Jones'?"

"It's not something I'm proud of, Julia. We had a fling on a dig in Mexico eight years ago. It ended badly with me being stupid. I never heard from him again. End of story."

Julia's eyes narrowed. "It seems to me that's all the reason you need to go out there. Because, clearly, it isn't the end of the story. You've got unfinished business with him."

"I would not be going to finish any…business. I'd be going for a consultation on this artifact."

"You could do that with a scanner and an e-mail."

Which was, of course, the truth. "See, that's why I like you, Julia. You never give me any BS. You just shoot me right in the forehead and get it over with, nice and clean."

"That's what friends are for," Julia said virtuously, snagging another wonton. "So, when are you leaving?"

"The conference is next weekend. I'd have to fly into San Jose. The conference people have a shuttle for the trip down to Big Sur, so I wouldn't have to rent a car."

"Big Sur? That's about as romantic a destination as you could wish for."

"Not for me," Cate said with firmness. "If I went, it would be strictly business. My extracurricular activities would be limited to discussions about cross-bedded sandstone and phallic symbolism in Mycenaean art with my colleagues in the field."

Julia snorted. "Ha! Beds and phalluses. What did I tell you?"

"That's not what I said."

"It's what you meant, though. Tell me honestly, Cate. When was the last time you had a mind-blowing sexual experience?"

Cate studied the wine in her glass, the pale gold of spring sunshine in California. She trusted Julia, honestly she did, but how did you own up to something like this?

"Um…I can't say I ever have. Sex just isn't something I enjoy."

Julia's aristocratic dark eyebrows said everything her closed lips were holding back, for which Cate was grateful.

"I've had boyfriends, of course. That guy Robert you set me up with two years ago, for one. And a couple of others—a visiting history lecturer, and most recently a disaster with the acting head of the anthropology department. He's gone to Northwestern now, thank God. But most of them just kind of…fade for lack of interest, I guess."

"Now I'm seeing why you're so successful in your field," Julia said. "And why your publication rate is double that of your cohorts in the department."

"Is that a bad thing?" Cate wanted to know. "If a man has that kind of publication rate, nobody says it's because he doesn't have a love life. They say he's ambitious. Which I am, and proud of it."

"Oh, I didn't say it was because of your love life. But I can see where all your sexual energy is going. Into your career. Which is why I repeat, go to California. Confront the wicked specter from your past. Put it to bed, as it were. And if it happens to be more than a metaphorical bed, then more power to you."

"You're supposed to be talking me out of this," Cate moaned.

"As your friend, it's my duty to make—er, encourage you to do what's best for you. And clearly, if this guy has been under your skin all this time, you have to do something about him. Lance him like a boil, babe."

Cate made a face. "With all that education, I'd think you could pick a better simile."

"It gets the point across, though, doesn't it? So, are you going?"

"Yes, I think so," Cate said with a sigh and a big gulp of wine. "California, here I come."

DANIEL WAS SO USED TO BEING in the spotlight that it was getting almost comfortable. Media darling, he knew, was a notoriously short career choice, so he didn't take it too seriously. But in the eyes of his colleagues, sometimes this insouciance came off as arrogance. Too bad. He couldn't help what people thought. What counted to him was the pursuit of knowledge, and people's opinions didn't concern him.

"Ladies and gentlemen, good evening," he said into the microphone on the podium. His voice boomed through the auditorium, reaching every one of the three hundred or so professionals seated eight to a table and enjoying the last of their dessert. "My name is Daniel Burke, and I'd like to talk to you tonight about the ancient treasures I've had the privilege of working with, as described in my new book, *Lost Treasures of the World*."

Fifteen minutes into his thirty-minute speech, the doors at the back opened and a woman slipped in. Slender and a little on the rangy side, she was wearing a black skirt and a white shirt that crossed in front and tied at the waist. She tossed back her hair and in that movement, so common and yet so completely unique to one particular woman, he recognized who it was.

His speech stumbled to a halt as she slid into an empty chair at a table three-quarters of the way back.

Cate Wells. By all the gods he'd ever dug out of the earth, it was Cate Wells.

He'd thought she was at Vandenberg, that tony private university with the seemingly limitless funding. Out there in New York, locked in an ivory tower on a different planet than the one he lived on. Not walking back into his life as inexplicably as she'd run out of it eight years before.

The audience rustled in its seats and he realized he hadn't spoken in some endless stretch of time. God, what had he just been saying? He glanced down at his outline, but the orderly print looked jumbled, as foreign as any Phoenician chicken scratch on a piece of clay.

Cate Wells.

Someone in the front cleared his throat and Daniel's brain snapped back into professional mode. "The expedition to Argentina and my subsequent discovery of the Temecula Treasure was the result of a domino effect of good luck and careful planning," he said, beginning part five as though nothing had happened.

Fifteen minutes later, the speech was done and he was striding off the stage to applause so tumultuous he couldn't hear what Dr. Purvis, the conference chair, was saying to him as she shook his hand. Her lips moved. *Sign boobs?*

That couldn't be right.

Books. *Sign books.*

Oh, right. A book signing was to follow his speech, out on the terrace where they were serving yet more gallons of terrific California wine. He hoped there were a few terrific California brews out there, too, or he was going to have to sneak off to his cottage and raid his own stash of pale ale.

Fortunately Stacy Mills, the publicity person his publisher had assigned to him, had taken note of his preferences, and a cold one was waiting for him at the table, along with a pitcher of ice water and a stack of books behind which an army could have barricaded itself.

Sheesh. Did they expect that every single attendee would buy one? Not that that was a bad thing. But it had already hit the *New York Times* nonfiction bestseller list, and he figured that in that case, everyone who wanted one would have bought it by now.

And speaking of Stacy Mills, here she was, with a dark-haired woman in tow. He handed a signed book to Andy Hoogbeck, one of the other speakers, and smiled at the newcomers.

"Getting writer's cramp?" Stacy asked. "Take a break. I want you to meet Melanie Savage."

With relief, he stood up and shook the woman's hand. "You'll have to forgive me. The name's familiar, but I can't remember where we met."

Her hair was cropped short and tinted with that dark purple stuff the Goths liked, and there was a discreet stud in her nose. Still, her face had an appealing heart shape and her eyes were wide and dark, and looked at the moment as if she were staring, dazzled, into a spotlight.

A fan. Daniel smothered a sigh and glanced at his line, which seemed to be lengthening again.

"We haven't actually met," she said a little breathlessly. "But I maintain your Web site, derringburke.com."

"I have a Web site?" He looked at Stacy for help.

"You have three or four. But Melanie here has the most comprehensive of your fan sites. Its name is a play on *derring-do,* Daniel."

A light went on in his brain. "Is that the one that wanted letters from me? For a blog or something?"

If it were possible, Melanie lit up even more. "Yes! You sent one a month for a couple of months. We got a zillion hits because of course it meant you'd singled us out to be your authorized site."

He hadn't—Stacy had probably sent him the request—but he wasn't about to dim that glow, especially if this girl's site was getting a zillion hits. Hits were good. Hits meant recognition of his work, and he was all for that.

"I'm glad it was a success," he said with his best ladykiller grin. "Nice to meet you, Melanie. And now—" he glanced at the line "—I'd better get back to work."

He signed copy after copy until his hand, rough and deeply tanned from holding its normal tools, a trowel and brush, was aching. But the wall of books diminished with every copy, until he could see over it enough to observe that the end was near.

And there, like the pot of gold at the end of the rainbow, was Cate Wells.

This was going to be fun.

"Who should I sign it to?" he asked as politely as he'd

just done at least a hundred times. As if she were any fan at any book signing whom he didn't know.

The smile that curved her lips held equal parts expectancy and irony. At his words, it tilted off her mouth and disappeared.

"To Anne," she said clearly. "With an *e.*"

Not Cate with a *C?* The name he'd doodled in the margins of his papers for years until he'd finally forced himself to quit? Instead of the requested *Anne,* he wrote *Cate,* with a *C,* and scribbled a line below it, then closed the book and held it out to her.

"There you are, Anne," he said. "I hope you enjoy it."

"Oh, I won't be reading it," she snapped, jerking the book from his hand. "It's for someone else." She marched to the cash register set up inside as if buying the book were a personal affront, one she'd been forced into under duress, and he smothered a smile as he turned to his next reader.

Conferences usually bored him to the point of unconsciousness. But not this one. He'd thrown down the glove and she'd kicked it out of the arena. She hadn't changed one bit in eight years. Still as uptight and brilliant and beautiful as ever. Her hands were still ringless. Her mouth was still that combination of innocence and carnality that could drive a man mad.

This was going to be one conference where nobody was sleeping.

Unless it was together.

FOR CATE, THE INSCRIPTION read. *May you find your buried treasure someday. Daniel.*

Cate tossed the book on the nightstand in her room, where its impact made the clock radio jump.

Just what the hell was that supposed to mean? Was it some sort of competitive gibe about the fact that she spent more time in the classroom than the field? Or was it more personal?

"As if you'd know what any women's treasure is, you slinking coyote." Her glare should have burned the cover right off the wretched book, but it just sat there, a sepia map of the "here be dragons" variety behind his name, which was displayed in at least thirty-point font. Above the title, as if he were somebody famous.

She grabbed the book and shoved it in the drawer of the nightstand.

Her nighttime routine of shower, moisturizer and hair brushing calmed her a little. Her body clock was set three hours ahead, so she was definitely ready to climb under the puffy duvet and shut her brain off for a few hours.

Tomorrow she'd figure out how to get a copy of the wretched book signed to Anne without actually having to see its author. Maybe the conference chair could arrange it.

She'd just glanced at the clock radio and noted that it was one in the morning her time, when a soft knock came at the door.

Who on earth…?

It had to be one of the staff, coming to see if she needed anything. At dinner she had recognized one or two people by name, and a few more by reputation, but none of them were on the kind of footing that would allow them to come visiting this late in the evening.

Ah well. She could use an iron for her outfit for tomorrow. She swung the door open and took a breath to ask for it.

The breath froze in her throat.

"Can I borrow some toothpaste?" Daniel Burke said with an infuriating, I'm-so-sexy grin.

4

"No." CATE TRIED TO SLAM the door, but Daniel jammed his foot in the opening before she could.

"Come on, Cate." The laughter he couldn't keep out of his voice made her face tighten up, as though she wanted to grab the door and bash it into his foot as hard as she could.

"Sorry, you have the wrong person. The name is Anne."

"All right, so it was a bad joke. I apologize. Come on, let me in."

"What for?"

He winced at the implication that there was nothing left between them to do, say or even think about. "I just wanted to say hello. Catch up on what you've been doing. Which is going to be really hard out here in the hallway, whispering to you through the keyhole."

"I don't have a keyhole. I use a key card."

He laughed. "I forgot how literal you are. Please, Cate. Just for a minute."

The Cate Wells he'd known in Mexico would have been a terrible poker player. Her emotions were mirrored on a face so expressive she'd once accused him of reading her mind. Somehow in the past eight years she'd learned to school it, to paste on a calm mask that hid what she was really thinking. Now that mask slid into place and she released her death grip on the door handle.

"Great," she said politely. "Let's catch up." She led the way into the room as though she were wearing designer shoes and a cocktail dress, not cotton pj's and a pair of bunny slippers.

He resisted the urge to comment.

She offered him the chair in front of the desk and he pulled it out and straddled it backward. She perched on the end of the bed, her jammies and bunny slippers at odds with the woman he remembered. The one who hung on rocks over fathoms of air and laughed. The one who put in hours in the broiling sun and counted it time well spent when she triumphantly held up a potsherd, its white-and-ocher paint faded by the passing centuries.

The one he'd thought he might be in love with.

The one who had run away.

He shook away the memories and concentrated on the reality. "You're looking well." Even the sexless cotton pajamas couldn't hide the fit, slender body underneath. He wondered if her skin was still as soft, and if she still favored skinny little midriff-baring tank tops with no bra when she was out in the field.

"That's hardly relevant, Daniel."

Visions of tank tops fizzled in his head. "You're supposed to say 'thank you, so are you.' Then I say, 'Nice paper on the feminine in that leopard cult,' and you say, 'Congratulations on hitting the *Times* list, I'm so proud of you,' and I say—"

"I had no idea your book hit the *Times* list. I'm afraid I don't pay much attention to that kind of thing."

As putdowns went, that was about as devastating a delivery as he'd ever heard. He studied her for a moment.

"Somehow I'd hoped our reunion would be a little friendlier than this."

"I didn't come here for a reunion. I came here for the conference and to consult with you about something. And what do I find?" She stood and began to pace around the room. "I find a man who is so full of himself he expects every woman in the room to swoon, no matter how rudely he treats them. I find someone who happily hogs the spotlight, presenting science as though it's some kind of entertaining reality show. And worst of all—" she took a breath "—I find someone who isn't above hurting and insulting people from his past, who finds it amusing to poke fun at them, confident that no one knows what he's talking about. Well, here's a news flash, Daniel." She marched over and stood squarely in front of him, her face flushed and her breath coming fast. "I knew you when you were nothing but a grubby undergrad who couldn't tell a potsherd from a shark's tooth and who, in fact, presented a lovely tooth to the class and proclaimed it was Anasazi pottery!"

Oh, God. The embarrassment of that moment flooded his memory—the snorting laughter of the supervising professor, the derision of the students for days afterward, and Cate's red face as she suffered through the moment on his behalf.

Back then, she had cared. Or so he'd thought.

"Do you suppose anybody remembers that?" he asked softly. And more important, did she remember what had happened afterward?

Later, when dinner was over and people were wandering back to their tents to moan over the no-alcohol rule, he had slipped away to the cliffs and found her sitting under a piñon pine, her back to the sandstone and her feet hanging over a hundred-foot cliff as if it were the deck of a swimming pool.

That night, the moon had witnessed their first kiss.

She was looking at him as though trying to see under the surface of his skin. "I doubt it," she said at last. "They've probably all bought your book so they can brag about how they knew you when."

"Except you."

"I bought it. Tonight. For my friend Anne. And you made a mistake in the inscription."

No, he hadn't. "I'll give you another copy for your friend and sign it properly this time." He stood and returned the chair to its place in front of the desk. "I was being an ass. Forgive me?"

Every time he moved, she made sure the distance between them stayed the same. He wondered what she'd do if he crowded her up against the sliding glass door. Her room was on the second floor of the main lodge, and he had no doubt that she'd probably rappel over the balcony, bunny slippers and all, if he tried it.

Instead of answering his question, she asked one of her own. "Who are you now, really, Daniel?"

He took refuge in flippancy. "The 'real Indiana Jones,' according to *Newsweek.*"

"Yes, I read that, too. But I'm more interested in what you think, not what *Newsweek* thinks."

"I could ask you the same question. I could ask why a successful, attractive associate prof is still single. I could ask why you prefer pajamas to, say, Victoria's Secret. And I could ask what I really want to know, which is why do your bunny slippers have teeth?"

Waggling a foot, she pretended to admire one slipper the way a woman admires a huge diamond ring. "They're a feminist reaction to male control of the sexual arena commonly known as the bedroom."

He stepped back, alarmed, and for the first time, her eyes warmed and her face lit with a grin. "You're not a Monty Python fan, I take it."

He shook his head. "You know me. The Webslinger's my man. Always has been."

"Some day I'll explain it to you."

"How about tomorrow? Over breakfast, say? We can talk about why you like teeth and I like crime fighters."

"I'm going for a run first thing."

"I'll wait. Some geology guy from San Jose State is talking about the mammoth bones he discovered in a riverbed. Not really my thing, so breakfast together would be a good alternative."

"Let's see how it works out. Good night, Daniel."

And somehow—he wasn't sure how—he found himself out in the hallway without even a kiss, while the door closed quietly between them.

In the morning, Cate proved just as elusive. When she didn't answer his seven o'clock knock at the door and she wasn't in the common room swilling strong coffee

with a lot of milk—was that still her drug of choice?—
he decided to mosey on down to the beach. True, she
could have decided that a run under the trees where the
road in to the conference center ran through five miles
of thick Monterey pine and live oak, was a good idea,
but he doubted it. The woman he remembered would
have headed to where there was space and light. In the
absence of hundred-foot cliffs, he'd bet she was already
a mile down the beach.

He'd have lost his bet, as it turned out. Big Sur was
famous for plunging cliffs and crashing breakers, and
the beach below the conference center was about fifty
yards long and mostly submerged under high tide. A
thin ribbon of sand was still left at the base of the cliffs,
though. Enough to give a woman access to—aha.

Cate Wells sat on a ledge about forty feet up, her legs
dangling in empty space in exactly the way he remembered. The ledge wasn't very wide, but she made it look
as though she were draped on a chaise longue poolside
at the Beverly Hills Hotel.

With a grin, he parked himself on a grassy patch at the
side of the path down to the cove, and watched her. Did
she do this at home in New York? Did she have days when
she thought, *Gee, I'd like some air—I think I'll go climb
out on one of the Woolworth building's windowsills.* Or
did she do what normal people did, and go find a climbing
wall at the nearest sporting-goods store? More important,
did she have a climbing buddy who partnered her? And
just who might that be? Some tight-assed stockbroker
who thought everything revolved around him? Who only
went out on windowsills when the market dipped?

There must be a man in her life somewhere. A woman like Cate wouldn't be alone. But if there was, how come he wasn't with her? Was he some kind of stay-at-home guy who did all her cooking and let her boss him around in bed?

A rock dug into his hip and Daniel got to his feet, feeling a little less cheerful than he had a few minutes ago. The movement attracted her attention. Cate's gaze swung from the pale horizon to him, and he lifted one hand in a wave. She waved back, turned to the side and began climbing down.

Watching Cate descend a cliff without equipment was like being six again and watching the trapeze artists at the circus. He knew she was capable. He knew it wasn't a vertical slope and she had plenty of handholds. But still, he didn't really breathe properly until she'd dropped lightly to the sand and begun the walk up to where he stood.

"Good morning." She loped up the slope and joined him where he once again lounged on the grassy patch overlooking the sea.

"I thought I'd find you down here," he said, "though I was thinking beach, not cliff. Have a seat."

"Couldn't resist." She flopped down next to him. "I feel as though I've been cooped up in my office for months."

"The academic year is almost over. Got any field-work scheduled for the summer?"

She refashioned her ponytail and stretched out those long legs. The way she leaned back on both hands thrust her small breasts into prominence. She was a line of lean strength mixed with an elusive sense of vulnerability that made him want to pull her into his arms and find out what was wrong.

For which she'd probably send him over the cliff.

"I've been working pretty hard," she said. "I was asked to assist on a site in New Mexico, but a friend of mine—Anne—" she shot him a sidelong glance "—wants to do a literary tour of England and asked if I'd be interested. I need to make up my mind soon."

"That sounds like a snooze. Here I thought you'd be dragging your boyfriend up El Capitan or something." The granite dome in Yosemite National Park was a magnet for rock climbers. He'd heard you had to schedule your climb the way golfers had to schedule their tee times.

"I'm between those at the moment." Her tone was calm as she looked out over the ocean instead of at him, but her jaw was tight. "Besides, I've already done El Cap."

"I'm sure you have. Not to mention every other rock face on this continent. You're going to have to widen your range to Europe at this rate."

With a smile, she said, "Maybe. I wonder if I can find Anne some literary sites in Switzerland."

"So what is it about climbing, anyway? Do you just like being on top?"

Her expression didn't change, but in the clear morning light it was hard to miss the hot color washing into her cheeks. "Does that threaten you?" she asked.

"A woman on top? Not a bit. I'm a big fan of that, in fact."

"I didn't know rock climbing interested you so much."

He grinned, that patented you-slay-me grin that studio audiences ate up. "Oh, I wasn't talking about rocks."

This time she looked at him full in the face. "If you're trying to embarrass me by making sexual innuendos, it isn't working."

"Liar. Who's blushing? Not me."

"I can't help my physiological reactions."

"I love it when you talk geek, Cate."

Abruptly, she got up and dusted off the back of her khaki shorts. "Clearly it's impossible to have a conversation with you that doesn't revolve around your two favorite subjects—yourself and sex. It probably works very well with your groupies but I need a little more mental stimulation."

She was already five strides away by the time he got up, and he had to jog to catch her.

"Cate." He swung her around by one arm. "Hey. Don't go."

"I want a cup of coffee." She pulled away and kept walking.

"Let me buy you one."

"I don't think so, Daniel."

"Come on. You can't avoid me all conference."

"I can do a fine impression of it." Her pace didn't slow one bit. They were leaving the cut through which the river ran and would soon be on the conference center's lawn.

"What about that consultation you wanted?"

That got her. She slowed. "Right. The photographs."

"We can grab some breakfast and take it up to your room, if you want."

"I don't think that's—"

"We need to be able to talk freely." He threw down

his trump card. "Don't forget we're surrounded. If these photos are something really extraordinary, we don't want to give anyone the jump on it, so to speak, by overhearing our discussions."

Despite her reluctance, he could see her acknowledge the truth of that. "All right. Breakfast at my place."

Internally, he was grinning, though it didn't show on his face. "Race you to the coffee," was all he said.

He let her win.

For now.

5

I'LL HAVE MY COFFEE, SHOW HIM the photos, and get out of here. I can be back in New York in time for *The Late Show.*

It had been a mistake to come to the conference. Cate realized that now, standing in the breakfast line in front of tables heaped with freshly cut strawberries, melon and orange, along with trays of steaming eggs and plates artistically arranged with bagels and pastries. She chose fruit, carbs and protein with a careful eye to the food pyramid, and filled her tall travel mug with coffee and cream. *That part wasn't on the food pyramid, but we were talking the bare necessities for survival, here.*

Daniel took two of everything. *How he hung on to that narrow-waisted frame feeding it things like that was a mystery.*

Back in her room, she cleared off the round worktable, pulled up two chairs and waved him into one.

"Isn't this cozy." Fruit, eggs, sausage and biscuits disappeared with methodical rapidity. He glanced up. "Aren't you eating?"

"Yes, of course." It had been a long time since she'd seen a man eat with such gusto. *Did he do everything that way—charge into it with such focus and concen-*

tration? Maybe that was why he was so good at what he did. Maybe people like her stayed in the office and wrote the papers and people like him went out into the field and gave them something to write about.

He gave the magazines something to write about, too. One of the things he also enjoyed with gusto was women, and as much as she'd determined not to think about it, it was hard not to with him right here in the room. He had that quality that made female heads turn. It wasn't the dark eyes, or the sensual mouth or the stubbled jaw. It wasn't the way his hair fell on his forehead or the long-fingered hands holding knife and fork.

It was the way they all went together, creating a whole that was much more than the sum of its parts. She'd sensed that quality in him years ago—that sexual quality, that magnetic thing that tugged a woman deep inside and said, "Yum. Must have that for mate."

Maybe that was why she'd run. She'd been as green as a bean at a lot of things—sex, life, men, you name it. Maybe some instinct deep inside had perceived that she'd be engulfed in him and lose a self that wasn't completely formed yet, and that had prodded her out of the cavern and out of his life.

Was it that same instinct that was telling her now she'd better pack her bags—or else?

Or else what, exactly?

"So tell me what I'm going to be looking at," he suggested as he finished the last of his breakfast. He took their empty plates and set them outside in the hall, though technically this wasn't a hotel and she had every reason to believe the staff wouldn't be impressed.

But then, he'd probably charmed the support hose right off the staff and there was an entire fleet of them waiting in the nearest linen closet to take his dishes away.

She took a fortifying slug of coffee and pulled the manila envelope out of her briefcase. "A woman named Morgan Shaw came to my office last week to ask if I could tell her anything about a wooden box she'd found in her antique shop in Connecticut. The only thing I could say for sure was that it was made of bubinga and it was possible the carvings are contemporary with Egypt's Nineteenth Dynasty."

He spread the photos on the table and leaned on his elbows, studying them.

"As you know," she went on a little diffidently, "a number of desert cultures were engulfed by Egypt's expansion during that period. I wondered if this was one of them."

For five silent minutes he turned the force of his concentration on the eight-by-ten color photographs, looking from one to the other, putting one or two side by side, then separating them and pairing different ones.

Finally he sat back and reached for his coffee cup without looking at it, his gaze fixed on the pictures.

"Wow," he said.

"Photos don't do it justice," she offered. "When you actually hold the box, you see just how the carved images re-form and flow into one another. Every angle gives you a different perspective. It's eerie."

"What's inside?"

"That's just it. There doesn't seem to be a way to

open it. But Morgan says there's a compartment—she ran it through an X-ray machine."

"If there's a compartment, there must be a key." He glanced up. "You know how tricky the Egyptians were with secret entrances and doors in their pyramids and gravesites. It was a common practice that could have been part of this culture, too, though clearly it's not Egyptian."

"Any guesses as to who might have made it?"

"The symbology has elements of Egyptian art, so I'm thinking there might have been a bit of culture bleed before they were taken over completely. Which would mean a neighboring kingdom, and given the difficulty of agriculture deep in the desert away from the Nile, those are limited to the Manassites and the El Gibi."

"The Manassite symbology doesn't include rivers or river animals, like this crocodile." She pointed to a figure on the photo closest to her. "They were a herd-based culture."

"That leaves the El Gibi, about which we know hardly anything. Not even what they really called themselves. Kind of like the Navajo naming the Anasazi."

Cate nodded. "I'm sure they didn't call themselves the Old Ones." She picked up a photo and Daniel took the one beneath it, a shot of the box's lid. "But what I'd like to know most is—"

"Cate."

"What?" She looked up.

"Look at this."

Obediently, she looked at the shot of the top of the box. There was a bird and some river symbols and the harp she'd seen before when—

Wait a minute.

"They lock together," she said. "Like those Escher drawings, only more complicated."

"Look at the edges. They form the shape of a star." His tanned finger traced the outline, an area about the size of a fifty-cent piece. "And the middle is hollow. Or maybe, given the cultural bleed, it's a Ra symbol."

Cate remembered running her fingers along the channels made by that awl all those centuries ago. Someone had held the awl with strong, powerful hands. Hands like Daniel's.

No, no. Do not think about that.

"Who do you think the artist was?" She didn't expect him to have an answer, but talking about the box kept her focused on work instead of…other things.

"Impossible to say." He tapped the photos together and handed them to her. "But he—or she—had an unusual talent. And the person was no stranger to geometry, the way those pictograms fit together to form the star. So, probably an educated person. More than that, I couldn't tell you."

She slid the photos back into their envelope and replaced it in her briefcase. "Thanks for the help, Daniel. It's not much to go on, but at least it's something to give Morgan. She was pretty passionate about it."

"You know antique people. They get that way."

With a smile, she agreed. "At least she wasn't the usual crackpot that shows up on my doorstep with some wonderful find that turns out to be a fifty-year-old fake."

"Don't you hate that?" He pushed his chair back and stretched, the fabric of his shirt pulling taut over compact abs and the kind of chest that a woman could fall on in complete bliss. "With my work at the digs, I get the ones who are convinced the clay pot somebody's kid made in the forties is an example of primitive art."

"Pre-Columbian, at that."

"At least. If not Precambrian."

To her surprise, Cate found herself laughing along with him.

"I can't blame people, though," he said thoughtfully after a moment. "Isn't buried treasure a fantasy we have as kids? Look at me. I've never lost that fascination."

"I supposed I haven't, either," she confessed.

"That's why I wrote what I did when I signed your book," he said quietly. "Some things haven't changed."

Cate closed her briefcase and set it in the closet, taking her time about sliding the door shut. "A lot of things have," she said. "Most things, in fact."

"Have they?" His gaze changed from professional to speculative with one lazy blink. "You're more beautiful. You didn't have cheekbones like that at twenty. And there's more confidence in your eyes. Makes me wonder if it's all those publications that put it there, or some adoring stockbroker."

Cate felt the hot blood seething under her skin. Was it from irritation at his personal remarks, or something darker and more dangerous? Was he flirting with her? And if he was, how was she going to respond?

She hovered in the middle of the room, uncertain whether to take her seat opposite him at the little table, where he'd probably think she was dying for more personal observations, or to remain standing in the middle of the room, where maybe he'd take a hint and find a lecture to go to.

"Cate." His eyes laughed at her, though his face remained serious. "Come and sit down. We were going to catch up, remember?"

She couldn't sit down. She couldn't trust herself not to reach out and stroke his hand, or run her fingers up his sleeve. That same sexual magnetism that had enthralled her eight years ago hadn't lost any of its potency, and if she got too close she just might lose it and become another one of his…what was that word Anne had coined? Oh yes—*archaeologroupies*.

With a mental shudder, Cate forced herself to ignore the siren call of his pheromones and be sensible.

"I'm afraid not, Daniel," she said as steadily as she could. "The ten o'clock seminar starts in a few minutes and I don't want to miss it."

"You're not going to listen to old Andy Hogbreath? How much more do you need to know about fossils?"

Was that who the ten o'clock speaker was? "Dr. Hoogbeck is highly respected in his field," she said stiffly. "And I happen to be interested in the fossil beds I find when I'm excavating."

"Suit yourself." He shrugged, then shot her a wicked glance. "But when you feel like thinking about any other kind of bed, fossil or not, you know where to find me."

She didn't bother to reply as, laughing, he let himself out. She didn't need to. Because her scarlet face had given everything away.

DANIEL HAD NO INTENTION of taking in Dr. Hoogbeck's seminar, or of returning yet another persistent call from a think tank in New Mexico, or even of returning to his cottage to tackle some of the logistics for the Asia Minor expedition. Instead, he stopped by the dining room to refill his mug of coffee and took an unhurried stroll down the nearest walking trail. It led through a stand of live oaks, their holly-like leaves spiky and rustling above him. Long native grasses nodded on either side, and a small stand of redwoods gave a bit of dark contrast at the bottom of the slope.

Daniel couldn't remember the last time he'd been completely alone out in the woods. You'd think that at this point in his career, he could say at any time, "Hey, all you hangers-on, get outta here," and he'd have some peace. But no. The problem was, no one was hanging on. His students, his fellow academics, his crews—even Stacy Mills, his publicist—all of them had a job to do. He was like the well at which they all drew, to use a simile from the ancient world where his brain spent half its time. He provided the water, and they let their jars down, filled them and then took off to do what they needed to do.

It was bloody exhausting is what it was.

And here was Cate Wells, who couldn't wait to see the backside of him going out the door. Never let it be said she wanted to fill her jar at his expense—no, she had her own well, thank you very much, and she was quite happy standing in front of it so nobody else could come near.

Or was she?

He'd thrown out those little innuendos on purpose. A

woman who was comfortable with her sexuality would have taken him on and tossed them back—but Cate hadn't. She'd been exactly the same way in Mexico. She hadn't had the same experience that he'd found most women had by their sophomore year. In fact, the first time he'd kissed her, he'd wondered if it was her first time, period. It hadn't been—that much she'd confessed in one of their late-night conversations on the cliff—but it hadn't been the kiss of a woman who enjoyed doing the wild thing at every chance she got, either.

Far from it.

Had things changed? Except for a very interesting ring he'd swear was Georgian on the right fourth finger, she wore nothing on her hands. And that sense of self-awareness, of the knowledge that she was both desirable and desired, that some women wore like an ermine robe when they were committed in a loving relationship—well, that didn't seem to be there, either.

But who was he kidding? He was used to reading soil matrices. The women he came into contact with were usually totally up-front and wide open about what they wanted. There was none of the reserve and mystery that was so intriguing in Cate. That reserve had challenged him back when and it was challenging him now. It was the same way with a new site. Just the presence of ancient clay walls with the wind whistling through them, silently keeping their secrets, drove him mad until he could gently tease their stories out of them.

He'd only been half kidding about the beds when he'd left her room. Now he wasn't so sure he was kidding at all. The truth was he'd never gotten over Cate. Had never forgotten that last night, in the cave.

So yeah, she'd run out on him, taking her secrets with her. But that was then.

This, he thought, as he turned back up the path, away from the river he could hear behind the trees… this was now.

6

Dr. Hoogbeck had the gift of being able to send an audience into a state of complete catatonia, even after multiple cups of breakfast coffee.

Cate had told Daniel she was going to this presentation, so here she was, even though geologic fossilization processes were enough to put her out even without Dr. Hoogbeck's soothing monotone. But instead of making her fall asleep, his voice sent her to that beta zone where she could think.

Unfortunately, she wasn't thinking about useful things like feminine imagery in animal cults or the demise of desert kingdoms. No, she was thinking about Daniel.

Because the simple truth was that Julia had been right and Cate had unfinished business with him. She wasn't a quitter. You start a degree program and you get a certificate. You start a paper and you reach a publishable conclusion. You start a relationship and you expect it to go somewhere.

Okay, so that last was something over which she didn't have all the control, but the point was you couldn't just drop something and run away and not have it bug you for years.

At least, she couldn't.

Because she was now in her ninth year of wondering what sex with Daniel would have been like, and, to put it quite bluntly, it was driving her nuts. He was the root of erotic dreams that woke her in mid-orgasm in the middle of the night. He was the reason she had had such high expectations for Robert Novinsky and Charles Morton and probably the reason she had sabotaged relationships with both of them. It wasn't that she was sexually dysfunctional, exactly, but what if somehow Daniel was the key?

What if she did take him up on his blatant offers and made him put his money where his mouth was? Would that unlock her sexuality? Would it break down this dam that seemed to hold her back in relationships with other people? If she had sex with him, maybe that would be the "kick galvanic" that got her back on track again.

And aside from the therapeutic effects of sex with Daniel, maybe it was simply time to have a little fun.

Fun was not a word she usually used in conjunction with *sex*. In her experience, sex was comfort, it was payment of an obligation, it was fulfillment of someone's expectations…but it was very rarely fun. She had no doubt whatsoever that if a girl wanted to have great big dollops of fun with her sex, then Daniel was the guy to serve it up to her.

What would be wrong with having a little fling with him? It wasn't as though he ever went into a relationship with the long term in mind. The endless string of girlfriends he'd paraded for the media over the years was proof of that. Not that she was keeping a scrapbook or anything, but every time she saw him in a circular for a benefit or in one of the scandal sheets, he was with a different "companion." If he wasn't going to commit to one of those beautiful and no doubt intelligent people, it was a safe bet he wouldn't expect anything from her, either.

Besides, it might be exciting to have an affair with someone who was the next thing to a movie star. The man every woman wanted. He was clearly interested. And she was mature and intelligent and on birth control. Why shouldn't she have a fling if she wanted to? It wasn't as if she would lose control and fall in love with him or anything. It wasn't like fieldwork, where the unexpected could throw your theories out the window or a freak storm could destroy months of work. She could have a fling under controlled conditions, having carefully chosen her subject, the way she might in the lab.

As long as she was the one controlling the conditions, what was there to be afraid of? There was no harm done to either of them, and they'd both enjoy it.

Cate straightened in her chair and slid her empty notebook back into her tote as Dr. Hoogbeck blinked owlishly under the stage lights, seeming a little bemused at the applause as he wound up his presentation. There was always the chance that she'd talk herself out of this, but at the moment it seemed like a fine plan.

Of course, once she'd made up her mind, Daniel decided not to cooperate. At lunch he sat at the faculty table, entertaining all six of his companions with some uproariously funny story that made heads turn and a little prick of envy at being left out needle its way through Cate's heart. He didn't go to the afternoon workshops, which made her wonder if that polished blonde who had been hovering behind him at the book signing was keeping him company in his private cottage, too.

It was merely speculation. Not jealousy. The man could have whomever he wanted in his cottage. But once she, Cate, had decided it should be herself, it was a little annoying to have him switch from being on her doorstep every time she turned around to playing hard to get.

She went to the afternoon seminar to hear the latest research on Cretan snake dancers to take her mind off him, and when she came out, there he was, walking under the oaks on the far side of the grounds.

He looked up when she was about fifty feet away. "Hey, Cate."

"Enjoying yourself?"

"Decompressing. I just spent the last hour with my publisher's rep, going over the plan of attack for flogging the book in Nevada and New Mexico. I need a drink."

"Your publisher's rep is here?"

"Yeah. Stacy Mills. Blonde. About this high." He held out a hand near his shoulder.

So she had been right. The polished blonde *had* been in his cottage with him. Plan of attack indeed. Attacking each other, more like. Cate's mood took a spiraling nosedive and crashed in flames.

"I won't disturb you, then." She turned on her heel, but before she could move more than a foot, he stopped her with a hand on her arm.

"Let's get out of here, Cate. All these people are driving me nuts. How about dinner?"

Her muscles jumped with anticipation under his hand, but she kept her voice calm. "Where? I didn't see anything on the way here but a café and some campgrounds."

"A couple of miles south there's a place called Nepenthe. Supposed to have a view off the terrace to die for, and good food. What do you say?"

An afternoon with his blond PR rep and now dinner with her? The man had stamina, she'd say that much for him. Well, she'd wanted a fling, hadn't she? If anyone was perfect for the part, it was Daniel Burke.

Cate ignored the little wail deep in her heart that reminded her of the heat and the connection they'd once had. Those days were gone forever. Some hot sex for a couple of nights was the key to her future, and nothing was going to stop her.

Even Daniel.

"That sounds great." She put as much heat as she knew how into her smile, and Daniel's gaze narrowed with interest. "How soon do you want to leave?"

AWAY FROM THE STUFFY ACADEMIC atmosphere of the conference and out of sight of their peers, Cate Wells seemed to have turned into a different woman.

She tilted her head back on the headrest of his 1968 Camaro ragtop and let the wind blow over her face. She looked as relaxed as she had on the cliff ledge this morning. More in her natural element.

And a natural Cate was all he could ask for.

Despite the fact that it was a Saturday night, it was too early in the season for the crowds of tourists that would flock to Nepenthe in the summer. The hostess directed them to a table on the edge of the terrace at his request, though the evening was cool.

Cate leaned on her elbows and gazed out into the vault of space between the plunging hills and the darkening sky. "I think I'll chuck my job at Vandenberg and come here and be a waitress," she said dreamily. "Look at that view."

He'd never seen that expression on her before—that sated, awestruck look that some women got after orgasm but that this one wore because of a view. He'd give a lot to know what she looked like in the afterglow. If it was anything like this, he wanted to see it.

"It's magical," he said.

"That it is."

"No, really. Nepenthe is supposed to be some kind of vortex—you know, the way Sedona is in Arizona."

"Why does it not surprise me that you'd bring me to a place like this?"

All her previous antagonism and chilly standoffishness seemed to have melted away, and her smile was as warm as the last rays of the sun as it dipped below the rim of the ocean far below. Maybe the ad copy was true and there was something a little…different about this place.

Maybe it was the atmosphere. Maybe it was the wine. Whatever it was, he didn't care. Because the Cate he'd known in the Mexican desert was back, sparkling and sexy and giving as good as she got. It wasn't even her face and body and that maddening mouth that had him gazing at her as spellbound as any high-school kid. It was her intelligence and the depth of her knowledge about the field they both loved that made him probe and parry, driving their conversation to where it had never gone before.

Neither of them had been ready for something like this before.

"I adore flan," she sighed at the end of the meal, licking the last of the caramel-coated custard off her spoon. "I got hooked on it in Mexico, but it's just not the same in New York. I think there must be something in the air out here."

"That's not a very scientific hypothesis." He grinned, enjoying the way she used her tongue to find every last molecule.

"Cooking is not science. Cooking is talent. And clearly, cooking at Nepenthe is a little magic as well. That was the best meal I've had in months. Maybe years."

"It's the best company I've had in months."

She waved the spoon in negation and put it on her plate. "Liar. I've seen who you've been keeping company with. Models. Starlets. Famous people."

"The trouble with famous faces is that's the only topic of conversation they have. Which is why I am a certified expert in moisturizer, with a secondary degree in depilatories."

Her giggle was a little high and a little fast, and he eyed the empty wine bottle. But given the choice between a slightly tipsy Cate and a frosty one hightailing it across the lawn, he'd pick the first one any day. But her stride was straight as she walked to the car after he'd paid the bill, and her eyes glowed as he took the curves of the highway with one hand on the wheel.

He parked in the conference center's lot and held the

passenger door as she got out. The night was cool but not uncomfortable, and over the ocean the stars winked in a sky as clear and dark as port wine. A breeze flirted with the branches of the trees overhead and the very air seemed charged with possibility.

"I don't want to go in," Cate said. She leaned on the door and crossed her arms. "If I go in, the night will be over."

Which was possibly the nicest thing a woman had ever said to him. "There's always the beach."

With a grin, she said, "Let's go."

"I DRAW THE LINE AT MOONLIGHT rock climbing," Daniel cautioned her as they walked side by side down the path, the scent of damp greenery and wet kelp in the air. "I've had too much wine for that."

"Don't worry. The beach is perfect." Cate flung out her arms as they reached the river and turned right. The path, though narrow, was well maintained and with the moonlight it was easy to find their way.

Cate felt as though she'd been transported into some alternate universe, where good food, good wine and the company of the man who had haunted her dreams for years were all it took to pull her out of herself. Because the real Cate Wells would not be running down a wooded path at midnight, laughing with Daniel Burke. She'd be tucked sensibly in her bed, getting the eight hours of sleep recommended by the National Institutes of Health.

Just for tonight, she was determined not to be that Cate. She was going to laugh and tease and tear off her blouse and wave it in the air if she felt like it, and no one was going to spoil her fun.

In fact, she thought as the path flattened out and led them onto the beach where the tide had gone out, she'd like it best of all if Daniel tore off her blouse and waved it in the air.

To get the process started, she took off her sandals and swung them on two fingers. "I haven't felt honest-to-goodness sand between my toes since I was in Spain. Our site was ten miles from the beach, so a friend and I would take the Jeep and go skinny-dipping in the Med."

"I'd have bought a ticket to see that." He took her other hand in his strong, rough one as they walked slowly down the gentle slope to where the waves smashed themselves into creamy oblivion.

"Why is it that people always walk to the waterline?" she mused. "No one ever walks on the beach and hugs the cliff."

"We're ninety percent water, aren't we? Maybe it's an element-calling-to-element thing."

"Maybe you're full of it." She tossed a grin at him. "Maybe it's just a good excuse for worn-out professionals to get their feet wet and feel like kids again."

"I'm far from worn out," he said with dignity. "How much time do you think we have before the tide comes back in?"

"There's a table posted on the back of my door. The people at this place are so helpful, aren't they? I think high tide is 3:00 a.m."

"Only in Big Sur do the tides matter more than the checkout time."

Only in Big Sur could she step carefully out of her old life for one weekend and become someone new. After all, wasn't that the promise of the Old West? You could leave your past behind and reinvent yourself as whomever you wanted to be. Here on the edge of the continent, she was going to uphold that proud tradition.

At least for these few days. Once her flight landed at LaGuardia, she'd go back to Vandenberg and care again about department politics and classes and getting the next grant. But tonight…tonight belonged to her and Daniel.

In the shadow of an outcrop that had likely once been an undersea bed of mud but was now twenty feet of shale, Daniel paused. "The wind isn't so strong here. Want to sit down?"

A prickle of anticipation tiptoed over the back of her neck. Sitting down was halfway to horizontal, and that was good. The New York Cate might have preferred to be horizontal in a bed with imported cotton sheets, but to the Cate who had been touched by California magic, the beach was perfect. In fact, where else could it be?

Daniel pulled her down beside him as a particularly big wave thundered in, throwing up spray lit by the moonlight. Legs stretched out, Cate leaned back on her hands and wondered if she needed to wait for him to make the first move, or if she should just push him down onto the sand and kiss him senseless.

One of her better plans. If she just—

"Cate." His eyes were lost in dark hollows as he turned to look at her.

"Yes?"

"Why did you run away, that night in the cave?"

And just like that, California Cate crumbled and she was twenty years old again, sitting in the dark with all her insecurities and fears coming between her and the one person to whom she could never reveal them.

Except…why couldn't she? What was the big deal? She didn't care what he thought of her. All she cared about was pushing him down on the sand and getting on with plan A. Right?

"Cate?"

"Because I was afraid."

"Of what? Me? Making love? Because that's what I wanted to do, you know. Make love to you."

"All of the above. You must know how attractive you are, Daniel."

He made a sound of derision, deep in his throat, and shook his head.

"I'm serious. You have this charisma, this thing about you that compels a woman to think about sex. To me— to the girl I was—it was overwhelming. I was afraid that if I let myself fall for you, I'd lose myself. I'd never find out who I was meant to be."

"Overlooking how this is making me feel, let me ask you this. You knew this at twenty?"

She shook her head. "Of course not. All I knew then was that I had to run. I got on the next shuttle out of there, even though I had a week left to go at the site. Of course, I had to write an extra paper to make up the chunk they were going to take out of my grade because of it."

"And all I knew was that you'd disappeared with no

explanation. And I was too proud to call later, when you got the post at Vandenberg. I was happy for you, though."

"I'm glad, though I can't say the same for you. Honestly, Daniel, do you have to encourage them to call you 'the real Indiana Jones'?"

He laughed and brought himself one notch closer to horizontal by rolling over on one elbow to watch her. Was his body language telling her something? At this rate, plan A was going to be a snap.

"I let the media call me that because it ramps up public awareness of what we're doing. And media attention brings in the grants. That's all I care about, Cate. Money means discovery. You can understand that."

She understood he cared less about public awareness than the media attention, but that was neither here nor there. Here was her opening. She let her gaze ramble over his face, down his neck, to the front of his shirt, where a couple of buttons were open. "Is that really all you care about?"

He caught her meaning immediately. "Not totally. You know me. Always a sucker for a challenge. Are you going to be a challenge, Cate?"

"What, another conquest? Another notch on your whip or whatever it is that you notch?"

The cocky grin faded and this time she knew she was looking at the real Daniel Burke, the one the cameras and the writers for *Newsweek* never saw. "You know it's not like that. You know you've been under my skin since that night in the cave." He reached out and ran his fingers up her arm, and an electric sensation sizzled through her blood. "The question is, are you going to run away again?"

Another wave crashed below them as the night seemed to hush waiting for her answer.

"Not this time," she said, and pushed him onto his back.

7

His body was solid with muscle and heated as though a furnace had been lit inside him. Cate planted her elbows in the sand on either side of his head and let her thighs fall where they would—as long as she had skin-to-trousers contact.

She smiled into his eyes. "Hello."

"Long time no see." His voice was soft, his eyes a heavy-lidded glitter in the dark. "Do you still kiss the same way?"

"How did I kiss?" She nuzzled the skin just above his collar. Slowly, her body was remembering how he had felt under her years ago. Remembering, and contrasting then with now. There was simply more of him. More muscle, more strength, more mileage…and more of that magnetic quality that promised a woman the ride of her life.

"I can't explain it," he whispered. "You'll have to show me again."

His lips welcomed hers. If she'd had any doubts about how they would fit together or if she'd forget how they'd once created such passion in their kisses, they were swept away.

Because, damn, he was better at this than he used to be.

She tilted her head a bit more and they fit together like two pieces from the same shattered pot, her curves fitting into his angles, her softness meeting his hardness. His tongue teased the sensitive surfaces of hers, wooing and tempting, drawing her in and making her forget her very surroundings. There was nothing in her consciousness but the heat and the taste of him and the wild rockets of desire going off in her blood.

His hands held her against him at the waist, then slid lower to cup her derriere and press her gently against the unmistakable bulge in his trousers. "Are you sure you don't want to go back up to my place?" he said against her lips.

"And waste all that time? Not a chance." She let her lips linger on his, learning the differences in texture and how each created a different response inside her.

"There," he whispered. "That's how you kiss. As if each one is a complete experience you might never have again."

"Is that bad?"

"Not at all. Try another one."

She tried one at the corner of his mouth, then she focused on that full lower lip. Unlike some men, Daniel didn't seem to think that kisses were like mile markers, flashing by on the highway to orgasm. He seemed content to let her explore and taste and even breathe in the scent of his skin as she rappelled slowly down his neck and nuzzled the intersection of throat and chest.

A man like this shouldn't be wasted on a fling. Cate squeezed her eyes shut and concentrated on the delicious abrasion of the hair on his chest against her cheek. On the way his rising heat triggered an escalation of her own desire. Because if she thought about the way she was using him, she wouldn't be able to continue—and right now, every cell in her body was demanding not only that but completion as well. She was the one barreling down the highway to orgasm, and it was all because of him and the chemistry that flared between them.

"I want to taste every inch of you," she murmured and went to work on the buttons of his shirt. He rolled to the side and helped her with the last two.

"Anything you want." She pulled the soft cotton out of the waistband of his pants, and he shrugged it off and laid it on the sand. "Now, what about this blouse?"

It was just a flowered bit of silk that had cost a fortune, even on the sale rack. With blissful male disregard for its label, Daniel pulled it off and the cool fabric slid along her arms in a farewell caress.

His mouth was hot on her skin, tracing the same path she had just forged on him. Was he having the same treacherous thoughts? Did making love with her mean a fling for him, too, or could there ever be anything more?

She might never know and right now was a bad time to figure it out. Because when he arrived at her throat, he continued down her body until the lace of her bra stopped him.

"Nice lingerie." His tongue on the curves of her breasts made her breath come faster, and when he reached around and unfastened her bra, the sudden relaxation of its fabric was like a surrender, taking her past a barrier she could scarcely admit was there. Out of the corner of her eye, she saw the fragile lace arc through the air to land on her sandals, and then she stopped caring because his lips had found her nipple.

The wet heat of his tongue abraded her sensitive areola and she arched up off his shirt, helplessly seeking more. He nibbled her flesh, rolling her nipple on his tongue until she lost herself in the sensation of it and the whimpering sounds she made were carried away on the breeze.

The muscles of his shoulders flexed and shifted under her hands as he moved along her cleavage and began his exploration of the other breast. Cate barely restrained herself from begging him not to prolong the trip—she needed his mouth on the other nipple *now*. But he made sure she enjoyed the journey, even though the anticipation she felt as he slowly circled and licked, nibbled and explored on the way to the apex had her gasping with the effort.

And then she had her reward—pleasure shimmered somewhere deep inside as he tugged gently right where she needed him to. Her body couldn't do anything but soften and moisten and melt.

He had made her feel this way on those warm nights in Mexico, too, but there had always been an undercurrent of guilt, of urgency, as though they were doing something wrong. Now that feeling was gone and she could give herself up to the pleasure as voluptuously as she wanted to. She was here on her own terms, she told herself firmly, with no second thoughts…and if Daniel made her feel a little out of control, a little bit over the edge, there was no one here to witness it but him.

When he lifted his mouth from her breasts, his eyes

were heavy-lidded and a little glassy, as though he were drugged. "I could just eat you up all night," he said, his voice ragged and soft.

"Please do." With a grin, she pushed him over onto his back. "But these jeans are stopping me."

"You could lose the skirt, too."

In moments they had all their clothes off and had fashioned a patchwork blanket out of them to keep most of the sand out of the way. Then Cate settled to the urgent and necessary task of tasting the skin on his stomach.

"Woman, you're going to kill me," Daniel choked as she swirled her tongue along the ridges and planes of his abs in exactly the same way he had tortured the curves of her breasts. When she applied a little pressure with her teeth, she could feel the tremors in his belly under her mouth, and smiled against his skin.

How delicious to know that she could do this to the famous Daniel Burke. She, Cate Wells, who had never licked a man's abs in her life, could make him tremble and harden with anticipation in the same way he had made her soften and gasp. Her body had never felt so alive, so conscious of every nuance of his breathing and the movement of his blood. Somehow it made her feel very sexy and powerful, and she forced herself not to think, not to analyze, but simply to move lower, just to see what he would do.

"Cate!" he ground out as she reached the junction where his abdomen met his thigh. His erection from this angle was huge and demanding and she held her breath. Whatever he was about to do was bound to be good.

"Enough." With one smooth movement, he rolled

her on top of him, so that he lay on the pool of clothes, his face a study in light and shadow, his eyes bottomless with desire. "You can't do that to me and get away with it."

"What will my punishment be?" she asked, torn between laughter and anticipation.

"Twenty lashes with wet kelp."

She grinned down at him, her hands on his chest. She'd wanted fun with her sex, hadn't she? Couldn't she be happy with that? "I have a better idea."

She was straddling his waist, and now she slid down until she could feel the rock-hard power of his erection between her thighs. Her entire body tensed with anticipation while the sensitive, slick tissues of her vulva caressed his length, teasing both him and her.

"You look like a goddess," he breathed, and her heart clenched at the expression in his eyes—as though he'd seen a vision, and that vision was herself.

"Everyone knows we goddesses like to be on top."

Balancing with one hand on the ground, she took him in her other hand and lifted up a little so she could stroke herself with the big, cushiony head of his penis.

"Ah, Cate…" Now even the muscles in his thighs were trembling, and she realized exactly how much it was costing him to let her take her time and explore not only her own responses, but his, as well.

She knew the mechanics of making love as well as any woman, but what she hadn't known was this sense of power that welled up at the same time as this helpless adoration of every play of light on his face, or this wonderful addiction to the scent and the heat of his skin. How was it possible for one woman's body to contain such a fountain of both physical and emotional sensation?

It was impossible. The first tremors of the impending explosion began to build deep inside her with the glorious, wet friction.

"Daniel, oh, I'm—"

Without a word and without interrupting their rhythm, he grabbed her at the waist and rolled her onto the mat of their clothes, and as the first waves of orgasm crashed through her, he slid into her body as if she had been waiting all these years just for him.

"Daniel!" she cried at the orchestra of new pleasure, as his length filled her emptiness, filled it, stretched it and made her body scream with the newness of it.

And yet, he didn't stop. Even as she shuddered and her mind tilted sideways, he thrust into her again and again, and she lifted her knees as if to pull him even deeper. It felt as though the atmosphere were bending, the beach were bucking, mimicking the tidal wave in her body. Daniel cried out and convulsed with his own release, dropping to his elbows to gasp an incoherent word into her ear.

But the waves kept coming. She'd never known an orgasm like this—it felt as if her whole body were still shaking and a sound like thunder roared in her ears. She'd known it would be good. But she'd had no idea that sex with Daniel would be such a cataclysm.

Daniel gasped something that turned into a shout and she finally realized what he had been trying to say. It wasn't her name, either.

"Earthquake!" He rolled off her body and pulled her

to her feet in one smooth motion. Her bones and muscles were still liquefied with the magnitude of what she'd just experienced, though, and she fell to her knees.

"Cate, get up! We have to get out of here."

The roar in her ears began to separate into terrifying components. The breakers foaming in lashed at the beach, thrown off their incoming rhythm by the lurching of the earth. A chunk of shale split off the cliff above them and crashed down not six feet away, impaling the sand. Beneath her knees she felt the beach still shuddering in the moment of tectonic release, in exactly the way she had with her own release thirty seconds ago.

"Cate, run! Get away from the cliff!"

Daniel grabbed her wrist and tugged her to her feet a second time. Together they staggered toward the waterline, the ground jerking so that every step landed a few inches away from where it was meant to go. They probably looked like a couple of drunks, walking a line that kept jumping out of the way.

Behind her, Cate heard a rumble that goosed her into a run. Wide-eyed, she looked over her shoulder.

"Daniel, the cliff! It's coming down!"

In the moonlight it looked as though the whole cliff had liquefied into a moving waterfall of stone. Cate's perception of reality wavered for a second—the cliff couldn't move like that, it wasn't possible—until she blinked and saw that the layers of shale were shearing off and sliding toward the beach, raining chunks as big as her body onto the sand where they'd been lying.

"My clothes!"

"Cate, no!" Daniel grabbed her around the waist and, stark naked, they stood at the waterline with cold ocean slapping their ankles angrily. Cate hardly felt it.

"The whole cliff. It came down right where we were—where we—"

"Were making love." Daniel's voice was soft but grim as he widened his stance and braced himself while he held her. The secondary seismic waves were fading even as they spoke, the way the vibrations of a train fade after it passes. "They'll be feeling this in San Francisco in a couple of seconds."

"Wow," she breathed. "It's been a long time. I'd forgotten what it was like."

"I didn't think they got these in New York."

She shook her head, her hair moving on her bare shoulders. She was beginning to feel sand in places where sand wasn't meant to go. "Not New York. At home in San Diego. Very frightening. Do you think it's over?"

"Hard to tell." He hugged her from behind, and she felt her courage coming back from where it lay flattened somewhere on the beach. "My guess is there will be some aftershocks. We need to get back to the lodge. It's not safe here, with all the falling rock."

"But our clothes! Not to mention my good shoes!"

He pulled back a little and looked at her. "You've just narrowly escaped death in true Indiana Jones fashion and you're worried about your shoes?"

Sheer relief at their escape mixed with a touch of hysteria as she erupted into unexpected laughter. "No, of course not. I'm worried about getting back to the conference center. Look at us. We're stark naked!"

"Yes, I had noticed that. You have the greatest ass of any woman I know. And your point?"

"Daniel, this is no time for jokes."

He grinned as he stepped forward to stand beside her. His fingers found hers in a tight grip. "We can't go near the cliff in case there's an aftershock and we get conked by another piece of falling rock. Our clothes will have to wait until it's safe."

"But how are we—"

"Stick with me, kid."

"Yeah, yeah, I know. And you'll buy me rocks as big as diamonds."

With a laugh that she'd remembered his old joke, he headed for the path on the other end of the beach, where the river had been carving its channel for centuries. She tightened her grip on his hand. He had a reputation for getting into and out of tight spots in the most flamboyant and newsworthy way possible. She'd buy a ticket to see him get her out of this one.

With her professional reputation—if not her clothes—intact.

ADRENALINE AND A KIND of savage joy coursed through Daniel's body as he and Cate navigated the path up the riverbed in the dark under the trees. He hardly felt the rocks and tree roots that crisscrossed their route, tripping up their feet and making the going difficult. Most of his consciousness was consumed with Cate. Making love to her, getting her out of the danger zone, getting her to safety.

Tonight was without a doubt the best night of his life.

To engage in foreplay over dinner—to have Cate respond to him in such an uninhibited way—to be able to give her the pleasure he'd been dreaming about for so many years—he grinned into the dark with sheer satisfaction.

An aftershock rolled under their feet, lifting and subsiding like a whale breaking the surface of the sea. It wasn't nearly as severe as he'd expected. Once he had Cate safe—and clothed—chances were good he'd be able to go back down to the beach to get their things without worrying about a chunk of rock taking him out.

They climbed the tree-covered slope that led to the grounds of the conference center, then stopped at the edge of the lawn, concealed in the shadows, to do a recon of the situation.

Cate hopped on one foot, picking something out of the sole of the other. "Why do those trees have to have prickles for leaves?" she complained in a whisper. "I think I've been permanently perforated."

"Want me to carry you the rest of the way?"

She put her foot to the ground and straightened, her body a pale length of determination. "No, thank you. I'd rather suffer under my own steam." Her gaze tracked the open space between their hiding place and the nearest building. "It's not that late. How am I going to get to my room without being seen?"

"I don't think you are. We'll go to my cottage and I'll lend you something."

"How come you get a cottage and the rest of us have to regress to dorms?"

"Because I'm the keynote speaker, remember? Plus they needed somewhere to keep all those cartons of books." He pointed. "I'm on the far side of the main lodge, up the path from the dining room."

"In other words, about as far from this nice dark tree as you could possibly get."

"Yeah, well, I didn't take earthquakes into account when I signed the contract. So we'll need to circle around on the high side—" he indicated the slope to their left "—and come down above the cottage."

"Why not go around to the right? It's shorter."

"That's the river side. We're more likely to run into people coming out of their rooms and stragglers from the night-owl sessions. People's instinct is to get outside when there's a shaker. And the lawn facing the river is nice and open. I'm betting everyone is already huddled out there."

She took a deep breath. "Okay. Point taken. My feet are never going to be the same."

"I'll give them a nice hot soak when we get to my room." He smiled and took her hand. "Come on. We're more likely to be spotted if we stay here."

He could have let go of her hand and had one more to navigate with in the dark, but she didn't seem inclined to ease up on her grip, either. Their feet made soft noises in the dried grass and leaves underfoot, blending in with the sound of the onshore breeze in the trees and the far-away boom of the ocean. It took them fifteen minutes of ducking and running, punctuated with curses as their bare feet found every rock on the hillside, before they slid to a halt under a pine twenty feet from his cottage.

"Can you see anyone?" Cate panted. She pulled her hand from his and pressed it to her chest, drawing his gaze to her bare breasts for about the twentieth time since they'd left the beach. It was a simple fact that he liked sex in the rough, and if ever there was an environment for someone with discovery fantasies, this was it.

Under the branches of a cedar, the cottage was dark and silent. He hadn't left any lights on, and the windows reflected the light of the waning moon. A big, round flowering bush of some kind blocked his view of the door, but from what he could see on either side of the little building, they were safe.

And Cate's body was a temptation he simply couldn't resist.

He stepped closer and slid his hands around her waist. "The only person I want to see is you, naked in the moonlight."

"What?"

He was so ready for her. His swollen erection nudged her derriere, then slid between her legs as he pulled her against him. "Who wants a mundane old bed? I want you up against this tree."

"Daniel, what about—oh."

He cupped her breasts in both hands and brushed his fingertips over her nipples. "You have the sweetest tits."

"Daniel, we can't," she gasped. "Oh, that feels so good."

Her flesh filled his hands with their warmth and fullness. He squeezed gently, pressing against her from behind, while she braced herself with both hands on the tree trunk. The arch in her back pressed her rigid nipples into his palms.

"Touch yourself," he whispered and licked her earlobe. "Tell me how wet you are." His tongue traced the edge of her ear and she shivered.

Hesitantly, she reached down, and he jumped as her fingers closed around his cock as it thrust between her legs. "Not me, baby. I know how ready I am. Tell me what you find."

Over her shoulder, he nuzzled her skin and fondled her breasts while he watched her fingers dip low and touch her cleft. "Mmm."

"Tell me." His whisper was getting ragged, and he held himself back from tipping up her hips and plunging into her.

"I'm all creamy and swollen," she said dreamily, "but that could be from last time."

His legs were trembling from the effort to control his excitement. "What does it feel like to touch yourself while I fondle you?"

"I like your tongue better," she confessed. "And I like it when you suck my nipples."

"You can have it later," he promised between clenched teeth, "but right now I want to slide inside you while you make yourself come."

"I want you to, too," she sighed.

"Tip your pretty little ass toward me, darling, that's it, and spread your legs."

Oh, God.

He gripped her hips and probed her swollen, wet lips, then slid into her. Her body clenched around him, then relaxed as he found a hot, slow rhythm. Stroking her breasts, he tried to give her as many sensations of pleasure as he could while his own body shouted with urgency.

"Daniel—Daniel—oh—"

He felt it almost before he heard her feathery little gasps. She shuddered against him and her entire body seemed to tighten and release around him as she came. At last he let himself go and the orgasm roared through him, blanking out the sounds of the night and leaving only the awareness of Cate and how her hips rammed against him as she took him even deeper.

He gathered her into his arms and he fell against the tree, its bark rough against his sensitized skin. "I can't stand up," he said a little helplessly, and took her with him to the ground.

He sat there for the few seconds it took to remember how to breathe, her body cradled against him so she wouldn't lie in the dirt and pine needles. He didn't care. In fact, the scent of pine needles was going to remind him forever of Cate. Probably when he was eighty and fetching a Christmas tree with his grandkids, he'd smell pine and get a hard-on, just from the memory of this moment.

A few moments passed and Cate stirred. "Remind me not to let you loose in a forest if this is what happens." Her voice was full of quiet satisfaction.

"It's the adrenaline." He adjusted her in his lap so she was more comfortable.

"Narrowly missing death is a big turn-on, I've heard," she agreed. "The urge to make sure the species doesn't die out."

"No, it wasn't that. Watching you running through the trees is what brought it on. You've spoiled me for ordinary beds now."

Her body shook gently as she chuckled. "That doesn't

mean I wouldn't appreciate one. After a shower." She got to her feet and checked the landscape around the cottage again, and he deduced that, while he'd be happy to sit out here and enjoy the afterglow as God intended it to be, she had other ideas. He got up and joined her.

"Come on," he said. "Let's make a run for it."

"Isn't it locked? Your keys are down on the beach with your pants, aren't they?"

He took her hand again. "Nah. We're out in the middle of nowhere and I've got nothing with me that anyone would want. Except maybe a few cartons of books. I left it open."

"You're more trusting than I am." She followed him across the grass, which felt soft and cool underfoot in comparison to the rough terrain they'd just crossed. "I never leave without locking my door, no matter where I am."

"You need to spend more time in the wide open spaces," he said over his shoulder as he turned the door handle. "You'd have more trust in your fellow man then."

He pushed the door open and slipped an arm around her waist, drawing her inside.

Had she ever made love in the shower? he wondered. And was it possible for a man to come three times in as many hours?

He couldn't wait to find out.

8

DANIEL FOUND CATE'S HAND and led her into the cottage. The moonlight coming through the south window lay on the floor in squares, giving them enough light to juke around the coffee table and make it into the bedroom without bodily harm.

"We could turn on a light." Cate's voice held laughter as she sat on the bed.

"There's lots of light in here." He joined her, pulling her down next to him on the duvet. "Enough for me to see how beautiful you are."

"I bet you say that to all the girls."

"Only when it's true."

"Daniel—" she began and stopped. "Is that someone at the door?"

He lifted his head from his concentration on just which breast he planned to nuzzle first. "Can't be. It's the middle of the night."

But sure enough, her ears were better than his. The knock sounded again, a rapid staccato on the wood.

"Don't move." He kissed her and rolled off the bed, snagging a pair of jeans out of his duffel on the way. At the door, he took a second to button the fly, then flipped the main interior light on and swung open the door.

The young woman on the porch smiled at him and adjusted the tote bag on her shoulder. She wore a denim skirt, black boots and a black T-shirt that said Wash Him and Bring Him to My Cabin in pirate-style calligraphy.

"Hi, Dr. Burke." She sounded confident, as if she were arriving for an appointment he'd forgotten about. That wasn't unusual, except he wasn't in the habit of making appointments at two in the morning.

She looked familiar, though. Cropped, purple-tinged hair. Nose stud. Big smile. The Web-site woman, that was it. But what the hell was her name?

Her eyes had locked on his naked chest.

"Is something wrong?" he asked finally.

"No, not at all." Her gaze traveled up to his face. "I hope I'm not disturbing you."

"It's two in the morning."

"I know, but we're both night owls. I've been keeping an eye on your cottage and saw movement, so I figured you were up."

Had been up. So to speak. "What do you mean, keeping an eye on the cottage?"

Instead of answering, she asked, "Can I come in?" And instead of waiting for the *No* he'd opened his mouth for, she slipped around him and parked herself on his couch.

"Miss—" Damn, what was her name?

"Melanie," she supplied. "Melanie Savage. We met the other night, remember? I do your Web site. And you can call me Mel."

"The only person I'm calling here is security unless you tell me what's going on."

Another big smile. "I came to the conference specifically to talk to you. You're a hard man to pin down. I wanted to do an interview for derringburke.com."

"Then you'll need to schedule it with my publicist, Stacy Mills." How was he going to get her off the couch and out the door without picking her up and tossing her?

"She hasn't returned my call. I prefer to go straight to the source, anyway."

"That's not how I work. Please go now. Wouldn't want you to miss out on your beauty sleep."

The girl's smile dimmed a couple of notches and became a little speculative. Her legs crossed at the knee, she sat comfortably in the corner of the couch, one arm relaxed along the back. Not the posture of a woman preparing to do as he asked.

"I don't need that much sleep. And I only have a couple of questions. Then I'll go."

Daniel resisted the urge to reach over, grab her and toss her out on her denim-clad rear. In the bedroom, Cate was totally silent and probably getting a chill. "All right. Two questions. Make it fast."

"Excellent." The grin snapped back onto her mouth, and she pulled a little tape recorder out of the tote bag sitting on the floor. She pushed the record button and set the unit on the coffee table.

"Tell your fans, Dr. Burke, the most terrifying moment of your career and how you overcame the fear."

"It's not exactly rock climbing, Ms. Savage. Digging in the dirt isn't that scary."

"I bet there was one moment, though. Tell me about it."

There was no getting out of this without resorting to physical violence. He resigned himself and spoke quickly. "Then that would be the moment when I realized Ian McPherson—you remember, the Canadian cabinet minister's son—had gone into the water alone to see that shipwreck. There were no guarantees we could find him, and he wasn't experienced enough with the equipment to be down there without a diving buddy."

"Was that worse than finding that leopard in your camp on the banks of the Amazon?"

That had been two years before the Temecula Treasure. Where had she dug up this stuff? "Of course. A human life was at stake. That's your two questions. Please go now."

"Just one thing—more of a comment, really. I want you to know how much your letters mean to me."

He stared at her. "What?"

"The letters you sent me." She waved a deprecating hand. "Oh, I know to the outside world there was nothing in them that couldn't go on the blog, but I know you, Daniel. I got your message."

"What message?" He barely remembered writing whatever she was talking about. In fact, his assistant had probably written them. She was pretty handy with a pen and had some talent at spinning facts into PR.

Melanie giggled as if he'd said something clever. "You're so funny. But you're right, there was more than one. It's the last one I mean, though. That's what got me on the plane out here. You said, 'Every time I journey back into the past I take you with me in spirit.'"

"I did?" He was going to have to have a word with his assistant.

"I know you meant that for me. So, here I am. Do with me as you will." Her eyes crinkled at the corners but the expression in them was very sexual. She uncrossed her legs and let them fall open, the message unmistakable.

Where was security when you needed them?

The light in the bedroom flipped on and Cate strode out like Peter Jackson's Galadriel having a really bad day. She had one of his T-shirts on and her cheeks were flushed with angry red.

Daniel stepped out of the way.

"I'll tell you what I'm going to do with you," she snapped at Melanie Savage. "Get off that couch. Now. And get out of here before I throw you out."

"Who the hell are you?" Melanie grabbed her recorder and put it in the tote, then clutched the latter to her chest.

"What do you care? Out!"

The woman stood and edged toward the door, her gaze swinging from Cate to Daniel. "You have a new girlfriend?" For the first time, her tone lost its assurance and stage sexiness. "What happened to that actress, Trisha Forrester?"

"None of your business. Good night, Ms. Savage." Daniel stood by the door as Cate crowded her across the room. Since Cate was three or four inches taller, it was pretty effective.

"But those actresses aren't your girlfriends," the woman protested. "Your dates are staged with them for publicity!" Her frantic gaze went to Cate. "He doesn't love you. He loves me!"

"He doesn't love either of us." Cate had her out on the path now. "Or your bloody Web site. Good night!"

In the light from inside, Melanie Savage looked shattered. "He could, if he'd give me a chance. You don't belong here, whoever you are. I've supported him for years. I deserve this, not you!"

"You are completely crazy," Cate informed her. She threw a glance back at Daniel. "Call security. The number is 888. Have her removed from the property."

Trust Cate to know not only the tide tables, but the resort emergency number, too. "Will do." He picked up the phone, but the gesture wasn't necessary. With a sound suspiciously like a sob, Melanie Savage fled into the night.

DANIEL CLOSED THE DOOR and gave Cate a grin that was half teasing and half admiring. "Nice job. Who needs security when you've got a T-shirt–wearing goddess on hand?"

Cate hadn't been aware she possessed a temper like this. Her chest felt as though it were about to explode and if she didn't find a way to get it under control, she was going to make a complete ass of herself.

It wasn't the unexpected visit. It wasn't even the fact that she was one of his archaeologroupies, because she'd known about them since the day Anne Walters had brought them to her attention by tossing a newspaper on her desk with a big picture on the front page of the entertainment section.

No, she was furious at the fact that Daniel was so well known for having affairs with every woman who threw herself at him that this girl—Melanie Savage, for Pete's sake, if that wasn't an alias, she didn't know what was—could walk in here with every confidence that her offer wouldn't be refused.

It was probably only because Cate was in line ahead of her that she'd been refused at all. Cate clenched her teeth so the roar of rage on the back of her tongue wouldn't get out.

"Cate?" Daniel tilted her chin with one hand while the other went around her waist to draw her closer. "She's gone. It's okay. Are you all right?"

She wrenched herself out of his grasp. "I'm fine."

"That's a woman's standard answer when everything is not fine."

"You would certainly know," she snapped, then wished she hadn't. *Get a grip, Cate. Act your age.*

She wasn't sure there was an age limit on jealousy. Because that's what this was. She was being jealous and unreasonable and she was ashamed of both. Because what on earth was she doing if not the exact same thing as Melanie Savage? She'd turned on the charm for Daniel and made herself just as sexually available, and he'd taken her up on it just as fast as she'd expected.

Daniel assumed she was angry with Melanie, but she wasn't. The truth was, she'd seen herself in the other woman—and the view wasn't pretty.

With a heroic effort at self-control, she turned to Daniel. "Didn't you promise me something to put on?"

His gaze was quizzical. "I wondered if you were getting chilly in the bedroom, but I needed to figure out how crazed she was."

"I don't think she was crazed at all."

One eyebrow went up. "You don't?"

"No. Her behavior was probably logical given the data she had."

Daniel narrowed his gaze as if he were trying to translate an ancient dialect. "What?"

She shook her head and looked past him into the bedroom. "If you're not going to lend me this T-shirt, maybe you could hike back down to the beach and get our stuff."

He tried to take her in his arms again, but she evaded him. "I was hoping we could dispense with the clothes, have a hot shower together, and go to bed."

"Yes, I know you were. But I don't think so."

"She really spoiled the mood, huh? Next time I'm not answering the door."

Men. She had no idea where people got the idea that they utilized their brains more efficiently. But as an excuse, it would do.

"Yes, you could say that. Besides, my key card was in the pocket of my skirt. Even if I did get back to my room dressed like this, I still couldn't get in."

He held up both hands. "I concede to your logic. But this isn't over, Cate."

Did he have to stand there, naked except for a pair of worn jeans, with the top button still undone? Did he have to have the most beautifully defined chest she'd ever had the pleasure of exploring, not to mention hips and thighs carved into leanness by his outdoor life?

She sighed and forced herself to look away. "No," she said at last, "I don't imagine it is."

He went into the bedroom and pulled on an ancient

brown T-shirt that said My Life Is on the Rocks. Two of the people in the anthropology department had brought back the same one after visiting New Mexico.

"Make yourself at home." He waved in the direction of an enormous gift basket filled with fruit, jars of jelly, chocolate and small bottles of liqueurs. "I haven't even opened that yet. Feel free. I can't take it home with me. And if I'm not back in half an hour, send out the search parties."

"I will."

Tossing an uncertain glance at her over his shoulder, he let himself out. When his footsteps faded, Cate tugged on the blue T-shirt she wore so that it fell farther down her thighs, and went to have a look at the basket.

It was a shame to spoil its beauty, but if he didn't plan to take it with him, someone may as well enjoy it. Besides, tucked in behind a box of biscotti was a bottle of chardonnay and two glasses. She found a bottle opener in the kitchenette and filled one.

The first few sips didn't do much, but three-quarters of the glass of cool, dry wine gave her attitude a chance to change.

She pulled the drapes on all the cottage's windows and, wine in hand, drifted slowly through its rooms. The conference certainly treated its speakers well. The dorms were comfortable, of course, but they didn't have washed pine furniture, or terra-cotta tile floors that made a cool contrast to the deep pile of the scatter rugs. Daniel's worktable was much bigger than hers, too. His computer was set up on one end next to his open briefcase, and the other end held a couple of the ubiquitous boxes of his books.

Good girls didn't look in other people's briefcases.

Virtuously, she turned away and walked into the bedroom to rifle his clothes. Well, maybe not rifle. She wouldn't even touch. But it was interesting to see that the rough-and-ready persona she'd seen on *The Jah-Redd Jones Show* was consistent. There were no silk suits and ostentatious ties hidden in the closet. Nope. Just a duffel bag with socks and underwear spilling out of it, along with a couple of pairs of jeans and some shirts and T-shirts.

He hadn't even brought a suit to deliver his keynote speech in—instead, he'd presented his paper in jeans. Even Indiana Jones put on his tweed jacket and horn-rimmed spectacles when he delivered his lectures, and goodness knows the man looked yummy in a tux when the occasion called for it.

You probably couldn't pay Daniel Burke to climb into a tux. He'd run screaming into the night, first.

With a smile, Cate turned back into the sitting room. As she passed the table, her elbow caught the upturned lid of the briefcase, spinning it around and sending it over the edge and onto the floor.

"Damn!"

Cate put her wineglass on the table and knelt to pick up the mess. Paper had sifted in every direction. She gathered it up, trying to keep typed sheets together in case he was proofing a paper. Maps, schedules, notes—well, there wasn't much she could do about that. She would just have to apologize and explain when he came back.

Reading glasses—the first sign that the he-man might have a flaw or two. Pens, pencils, a bottle of headache tablets, a digital camera. Good thing that had landed on the soft carpet. She would have had to replace it if it had smashed on the glossy tile.

She put the briefcase back on the table and began to put everything into it. When she finished, she realized that some of the things must have gone into the compartments in the lid, because there was something tucked in there that she hadn't noticed before.

A photograph.

She pulled it out, curious as to who would be so important to Daniel that he would keep it with him on his travels. His family? Or a girlfriend about whom the papers knew nothing?

She gazed at the photo and blinked.

It was herself.

She even remembered the day it had been taken. They'd knocked off early because a huge thunderstorm had blown up out of the east, sending everyone at the Mexican dig scurrying for shelter like the ground squirrels running for their holes. After the storm had passed, she had taken a walk out to her favorite aerie on the cliff to watch the clouds travel to the west. The setting sun had broken through them in bars of deep golden light, and the first inkling she'd had that she was not alone had been the click of the shutter as Daniel had snapped the picture behind her.

She'd never seen it, of course. Never seen any of the pictures he'd taken.

Daniel had caught her in profile, with the glorious sunset lighting one side of her face. God, she looked so young. So vulnerable and clueless about the world.

With the number of models and starlets in his life

helping him stay in the spotlight, why would he want to keep a picture of an ordinary academic close to him? It clearly went everywhere with him, tucked into the lid of his briefcase where the casual onlooker wouldn't see it behind other papers. Was it a reminder of some kind? A memento of a time before work and academia and the reality of making a living had set in?

Or was it something deeper than that?

Could Daniel possibly have cared much more than she'd thought? Could he still care?

No. Impossible. The starlets shot down that line of thinking before it even got off the ground. A man who cared would have contacted her at least once in eight years, even if it were just to ask why she'd left and whether she was interested. A man who cared would not have shrugged his shoulders and gone on to his merry string of camera-ready companions.

As she suspected, there was no analyzing the male mind. She needed to stick to plan A. A simple fling and then she would move on herself. Already she could feel the benefits of this therapeutic approach. She was loose-limbed and still glowing with the aftereffects of sex. A few more treatments at Daniel's hands and she'd be as good as new and ready for the next real relationship that came along.

No more uncertainty. No more fear.

And no more waiting around. Cate frowned at the clock over the kitchenette's sink. Daniel had been gone for half an hour and it certainly didn't take that long to hike down to the beach and back. Probably he'd run into the lovely Stacy Mills and gotten distracted.

Her brave mood punctured, Cate marched into the bedroom and snatched a pair of clean boxers out of Daniel's duffel. She'd have them laundered and return them in the morning. Meantime, she'd go to security and have them let her into her room.

Sometimes a woman just had to do things herself instead of forever waiting around for a man.

9

DANIEL HALF EXPECTED the beach to be destroyed as he jogged off the path and onto the sand. He moved slowly around the slices of rock that had broken off the cliff face, and kept one eye cocked upward in case there was an aftershock and something else—bushes, rocks, maybe even a tree—got jarred loose.

He'd often heard people describe sex as making the earth move, but he'd dismissed it as an overwrought metaphor. He'd never expected to experience the real thing. But then, what could he expect when it was Cate you were talking about? The fact was, earthquakes or not, she rocked his world and always had.

The sand was cold under his feet, the wind off the water chilly on his bare skin. He made his way around the rubble of fallen rock and tried to estimate where they had been lying when the North American and Pacific plates had decided to release their tension like a cataclysmic rubber band. He followed their footprints down the beach, and when he'd rounded a huge, freshly minted boulder, he saw the little heap of clothing lying in the sand.

Lucky thing he had good reflexes. The boulder had come to rest on the leg of his jeans.

He put his back into it and managed to lift the rock long enough to pull his pants out from under it, then scooped up his shirt and Cate's skirt and blouse. A touch of the pocket told him her key card was still safe. He turned to go and remembered one last thing.

Her shoes. God help him if he got back to the cottage and didn't have her shoes. With a smile at his austere Cate—who chased off rabid fans wearing nothing but a T-shirt—having such a feminine weakness, he looked around the beach more carefully.

Ah. There they were, behind another fallen rock, along with her bra. Lucky thing the moon hadn't set yet. He'd have had his work cut out for him, scrabbling around in the sand trying to find their things in pitch darkness. As he picked up the leather sandals and scraps of lace, something else caught his eye in the moonlight.

The cliff hadn't had that kind of relief before. Shale was smooth. He walked closer, alert for falling pieces, to get a better look.

Fossils. A vertebra, to be exact. And beside it, a jawbone, complete with teeth. Lots of them.

Daniel looked up. An entire layer of shale had been sheared off the way a knife slices through cake, revealing the layer that had been waiting beneath it. Millions of years ago these layers had been flat and deep under the ocean, but now, with tectonic movement, they had been upthrust until they were standing vertically. Ancient creatures that had sunk into the mud to die were now frozen in the cliff like a giant window into the past.

"Oh, my God." He climbed a couple of rocks, the

clothes clutched in one hand and Cate's sandals dangling from his fingers. "It's a whole skeleton."

Sure enough, he could clearly see a curved line of vertebrae and as many ribs. He had no idea what they were, but there was someone up there in the conference center who would. It wasn't a mammoth, like the one that was currently rewriting textbooks in that riverbed in San Jose. Maybe it was just a really big fish, or an ancient kind of whale. But in any case, his duty to his fellow academics was clear.

Paleogeology wasn't his bailiwick. But it was the love of Andy Hoogbeck's life.

Daniel hopped down to the sand and took off up the path at a run. When he cleared the trees, he saw that his earlier prediction had proved to be accurate. Most of the conference attendees were milling around on the dark lawn. Someone had brought out the booze and a portable radio, and it had turned into an impromptu cocktail party, with people standing around chatting in their pajamas and sweats.

Stacy Mills caught sight of him as he circled the crowd. "Daniel! Thank God you're all right." She clutched his arm, looking tousled and relatively human in her silk pj's and no makeup. "I can't go back in that building. I'm afraid the roof is going to come down."

He patted her hand and removed it gently. "Are they checking it out? Is that why everyone's out here?"

"Yes, the security people are doing a sweep to see if there's been any damage. What about your cottage? Is it all right?"

He hadn't even thought to look. "Yes, it's fine. Say, have you seen Dr. Hoogbeck? I need to ask him something."

"He's over there." She pointed toward the edge of the lawn. "I need a drink. I swear, I'm going to demand hazard pay for this."

He left her trying to coax another glass of wine out of someone and found Dr. Hoogbeck holding forth on the dynamics of earth movement to a small group of archaeologists. He interrupted the older man with a firm grip on his arm.

"Excuse me, Dr. Hoogbeck. I need to speak with you urgently."

"Is it about your cottage?" The paleogeologist came without protest and his relieved audience faded in the direction of the booze. "This facility is built on stone. I don't know what everyone is so worried about. I could have told those people—"

"Dr. Hoogbeck, the earthquake damaged the cliff down at the beach. There's something down there I think you should see."

Hoogbeck may have been a crusty old bore, but he was no fool. His bushy eyebrows rose. "Yes?"

Daniel leaned in so no one could overhear. "The cliff sheared away and you can clearly see vertebrae. A skeleton of some kind, maybe forty feet long."

"Are you sure?" All the pomposity and windy verbosity had blown off his mien in the space of a moment, leaving behind the avid scientist. "Where?"

Daniel glanced at the man's feet. "You've got shoes on? Good. Follow me."

He stashed his and Cate's clothes under a lawn chair

near the trees, where they'd be easy to retrieve, and he and the professor retraced his steps down to the beach. Cate would understand. If the fossils proved to be something unusual, the fact that he hadn't come right back would be easy to explain.

"Careful. If we get another aftershock we need to be out of range of falling rock." Dr. Hoogbeck followed Daniel to the freshly exposed face, and they both scrambled up on a boulder. Hoogbeck pulled a flashlight out of the pocket of his dressing gown and played it over the fossils.

A minute of silence ticked by. Then another. The flashlight beam traveled across and back. Across and back.

Daniel could stand it no longer. "Well?"

"This is amazing," Dr. Hoogbeck said in a hushed tone. "Such well-preserved specimens."

"What are they?"

"Vertebrae, as you said. It—it almost looks like an *Elasmosaurus platyurus*. A kind of plesiosaur. If the Loch Ness Monster were real, some believe this creature might have been related to it." The geologist glanced at him. "But of course such a thing must be confirmed with careful excavation and research. You'll have another fabulous find to add to your résumé, Dr. Burke. This one will rewrite the textbooks, too, along with our woolly friend in San Jose."

Daniel jumped off the rock and held up an arm to help the older man down. "Not me. I'm no rock guy. Give me pottery any day. That's why I came and got you. You take credit for the discovery and get all the work of excavating it, if it comes to that."

"You're pulling my leg." The older scientist stopped walking, his dressing gown blowing around his bony knees. "This could be huge. Why would you want to give it up?"

"Because it's not my field, and because I know you'll treat it with the respect it deserves. It's as simple as that."

"Total credit," the scientist repeated in disbelief.

"Mum's the word." Daniel could only imagine what the media would do with this if it got out that he had made the find. Adventurer Says Nessie Is Real! He could see the tabloids now. And wouldn't that be a nice side note— make that *sideshow*—to otherwise stellar research.

Side by side, they climbed the path up to the conference center. "In fact, I'll just go about my business once we get to the lawn, and you can announce the find tonight, before any early morning health fanatics find it tomorrow."

"I haven't had a major announcement in fifteen years," Dr. Hoogbeck said a little breathlessly as they reached the lawn. "I owe you for this, Burke. If there's anything I can ever do for you, you just name it."

"I'll keep that in mind, sir. Good luck."

He watched Hoogbeck hustle into the middle of the crowd, and turned away. He scooped up the little pile of clothes from under the lawn chair and jogged across the grounds to his cottage. A warm, low light shone from the windows in an understated welcome. Cate, of course. She'd even turned on the light beside the door.

It had been a long time since there had been anyone around to do such a thing for him. He was so used to coming home to a dark condo, whether staggering off a transatlantic flight or returning home from a local lecture, that he'd forgotten there were such things as home lights.

Not that this was home, but still.

If Cate is there, does that make it home?

He brushed off the thought with a smile and opened the door. "Hey, I'm back. You won't believe what I found when I got to the beach."

Silence echoed in the cottage. The bathroom and bedroom were both empty. Just to be sure, he looked behind the couch. "Cate? Are you here?"

But she wasn't.

Daniel flopped onto the couch, tossing their clothes and her shoes into the corner of it. That's when he saw the note on the coffee table, under an empty wineglass.

Not sure where you are so went back to my room. Enjoy the rest of the conference.

Daniel crumpled the note until he could no longer see the measured, tidy handwriting.

If that wasn't a brush-off, he didn't know what was.

Despite the fact that it was nearly three in the morning and he'd had two orgasms in the last three hours, Daniel couldn't relax enough to go to bed. He wanted to march over to the dorm and demand to know what Cate thought she was doing when it was clear they were supposed to have spent the night together in sleepy comfort.

But on the other hand, if she couldn't wait for half an hour or stick around to hear why he'd been delayed, why should he bother? He'd just go to sleep like the rational guy he was and let her make the next move…because he had no idea what was going on in her head.

IN THE MORNING CATE COULD hardly make her way to the coffee station in the cafeteria for the knots of people clogging the way, all talking about something that had happened last night after the earthquake. Lack of sleep had made her fuzzy-headed and she downed half a cup of excellent coffee before the excited conversation next to her at the table made any sense.

"Yes, he went down to the beach after the first temblor—at some risk, you understand, because of the falling rock," the blond historian across the table said to her companion. "And he found the bones then."

Had there been a murder? Cate tapped her on the shoulder. "Who found bones? And whose were they?"

The woman said, "Andy Hoogbeck. This will bring his career back to life for sure. He found the bones of a nearly complete plesiosaur in the cliff last night. A whole section of rock had sheared away and there they were."

Andy Hoogbeck had been on the beach last night? Good heavens, what had he seen?

Cate subsided into her own chair with a murmur of thanks and stared sightlessly at her raspberries and yogurt. She and Daniel had been on the beach, as naked as Adam and Eve, and doing what Adam and Eve had done best with their instructions to populate the earth. Granted, Dr. Hoogbeck was old, and it had been dark, and there was the earthquake…but…

Get a grip, Cate. Under those circumstances people think about saving their skins, not about voyeurism. Dr. Hoogbeck is not going to gossip about you doing the wild thing with Daniel Burke in a public place. It's not going to get back to the department chair and you're not going to be fired because of it. Calm down and eat your yogurt.

Maybe she'd ask him. Just to be sure. She couldn't go up and say, "Dr. H., did you see me having wild monkey sex on the beach last night?" She'd be more subtle than that. A lot more subtle.

She got her opportunity a few minutes later at the coffee station, when she got her second refill. Dr. Hoogbeck was drowning a teabag in a mug of hot water with the back of a spoon. There was no one within earshot.

"Good morning," she greeted him. "I hear great news about you this morning. Everyone is talking about it."

"Yes." He beamed at her in a grandfatherly sort of way. "I'm consulting with two of my colleagues in the field in a few minutes, as a matter of fact. The conference center will be hosting a press conference via satellite this afternoon at four o'clock. The main conference will be over by then, of course, so it won't disturb the proceedings."

"How exciting," Cate said. And it was, if you were a geologist. To her, bones were mildly interesting but not nearly a discovery on the scale of, say, a bit of stonework bearing a goddess figure.

"So what took you down to the beach in the middle of an earthquake?" she asked casually. If he was meeting colleagues in a few minutes, she didn't have the luxury of working up to it slowly. "Did you have a hunch?"

The older man nodded. "You never know with this coastline. It's as unpredictable as a beautiful woman." He smiled at her, and Cate gathered she was to take this as a compliment, though *unpredictable* was not a word anyone might apply to her. "Though Dr. Burke might disagree with me."

"Dr. Burke?" Cate repeated as a dart of apprehension shot through her.

"Yes, I saw him on the beach." He twinkled at her and Cate felt the bottom drop out of her stomach. "But you might know more about that than I. I noticed the two of you together when I was out for my walk the other morning."

"Dr. Hoogbeck, I must ask you not to—"

"Ah." He put his mug of cooling tea on the table and waved at two men in field gear at the door. "There are my colleagues. Please excuse me, Dr. Wells."

"But I—"

Too late. He was off across the dining hall, still carrying the teaspoon he'd been using on the teabag. Oh, dear. He'd seen Daniel and had been too polite to say aloud that he'd seen her, too, in all her naked glory. Was it too much to hope that he was shortsighted or something? Or that he knew how to hold his tongue?

Having a fling was one thing. Having a fling and finding out everyone in the academic world was talking about it was quite another. She couldn't risk even a whisper getting back to the dean at Vandenberg, who was one of the stuffiest people she'd ever met. She hadn't spent years laying the groundwork for early tenure just to lose it over something like this. Because it was an unhappy fact that everything Daniel Burke did got people whispering and talking.

Maybe she'd better find Daniel. There were two of them in this debacle, and chances were good he'd had more practice at damage control. It could certainly not be said that her life previous to this had anything in it worth gossiping about.

The last of the colloquia began at ten, and she checked every conference room without success. Daniel must be in his cottage, and if he wasn't there she'd just have to leave a message on his voice mail saying she needed to speak to him urgently.

In the face of this new disaster, the fact that he'd failed to come back last night faded into insignificance. She'd put aside speculation and petty jealousy, and focus on the important thing—gagging Dr. Hoogbeck.

But at her urgent knock, the cottage door swung open and there Daniel was. Without missing a beat, he looked at her empty hands curiously. "Did you bring the coffee?"

"Of course not. I have to talk to you."

"If it's about last night, I'm sorry I didn't get back here right away. It was pretty exciting, what with the—"

"Spare me the details of your conquests. I spoke with Dr. Hoogbeck just now and he saw us on the beach." She pushed past him and his eyebrows rose, but he said nothing as he closed the door behind her. "We have to figure out a way to keep him quiet."

"About what he found on the beach? I doubt even duct tape and a lip clamp would keep him quiet."

Cate held back a screech of frustration with her last reserves of self control. Of course he didn't care about her reputation. This kind of thing simply polished a man's. It was different for a woman, especially one like herself, with a lot more to lose.

"I know you couldn't care less about being seen with

yet another woman, but I care deeply. One word in the wrong ear and Dr. Hoogbeck could ruin me at Vandenberg. They have very strong feelings about the…what's that phrase…*moral rectitude* of their faculty."

Daniel waved his hands in the air as if flagging down a runaway horse. "Whoa, wait just a minute, Cate. What are you talking about?"

She threw her hands in the air. "I just told you! Dr. Hoogbeck saw us on the beach and you just said it would take more than duct tape to keep him quiet! Oooh, there's nothing worse than a man who doesn't even listen to his own conversations."

"That's because we're talking about two different things. I'm talking about the fossils. You're talking about us making love. Dr. Hoogbeck couldn't have seen that. I found him up on the lawn in his dressing gown, lecturing a group of people on tectonic movement."

"But then why did he say he'd seen us?"

"He saw me. Because I took him down there."

"He wanted to show you the fossils?"

"No, I wanted to show him. I found them when I went to get our clothes. The cliff had sheared away and he was the first person I thought to tell."

She stared at him. "You discovered them? Then why is Dr. Hoogbeck having the press conference and not you?"

Impossible. The Daniel Burke with whom she was having this fling would never give up a chance to get the media swarming all over him. He would never give credit for a major discovery to someone else and walk off into the night without making sure there was something in it for him.

Could she have been misjudging him all this time?

Did she want to have her fling with Daniel Burke the media creation? Or with Daniel Burke the man?

10

DANIEL TOOK CATE'S ARM and led her to the couch, where he pushed her into it gently then went to raid the gift basket. He snagged a bottle of amaretto, twisted off the top and handed it to her.

One hit off the little bottle had her coughing and choking, but it warmed her all the way down.

"Because," he answered her at last, "I told him to take the credit. Fossils are not my thing. They're the love of his life. And I kind of like the old codger. He has a good heart, if you give him a chance. This will keep him happy for months to come." He took the bottle from her and had some himself. "Besides, I'm sick to death of press conferences. If I had to do another one before the ones I have in San Francisco later in the week, I'd probably do something stupid, like moon the reporters or stagger into the room drunk. Not the best reflection on our fair discipline."

She took the bottle back and had another sip, with a little more control this time. Her mind was racing with questions—about herself, about him and about her own motives. "That's why you didn't come back here. You were down at the beach with him, showing him the fossils."

"And by the time I got back, you were gone."

She glanced at him, ashamed of herself. "I assumed you'd been waylaid by a blonde and forgotten...my shoes."

"Nope. And as for...your shoes, they're over there, on the chair with your things." He waved in the direction of the table. Sure enough, her Ferragamo sandals were sitting on one of the chairs, her skirt and blouse neatly folded on top of them.

Was his decision to sidestep the spotlight for once some kind of ploy—some kind of backward way of impressing her? Along the lines of *I'm so famous, I don't need any more attention?* Or was it as simple as he made it out to be? Fossils weren't his thing, so he turned the whole discovery over to someone who would appreciate them more. Game over. Move on.

"Daniel, just how much of the press about you is true?" And how many of her assumptions about him were true?

He got up and brought back the entire basket. Digging through it, he replied, "Some of it is true. *Newsweek* got the facts right, for instance. And everything I said to Jah-Redd was true. But the ragmags go for sales, not facts, so you have to take what they say with a grain of salt." He handed her a small package wrapped in gold foil. "Godiva?"

"Thank you. Are you going to take that whole basket apart?"

"It's meant to be eaten, isn't it? I figure we can hole up here for the rest of the day and not even have to go to the cafeteria. Look—fresh grapes."

He held one up and she opened her mouth. He slid

it between her lips and she bit down on it. Sweet juice exploded on her tongue. "Cabernet," she said around it. "Yum."

"You can tell what kind of grape it is by one taste?" He ate one himself and shrugged. "It tastes like a grape."

"You obviously didn't do the extra-credit work during your exchange semester."

"My loss." He fed her another. "You didn't learn about grapes in Mexico, I'll bet."

"No, we did a field excursion on prehistoric art in the south of France. And there was this Wine-making 101 type of class and I had a couple of weeks to play with at the end of the art class, so I took it."

"Cate, most normal people with a couple of weeks to spend in the south of France would go sunbathe naked on a beach, not take another class."

"I'm not most people." She leaned against his shoulder and peered into the basket. "What else have you got in there?"

"I have some cassis and some Kahlúa, and what seems to be a couple of fingers of Glenlivet."

"Yuck." She hated hard liquor and had ever since her freshman year in college, when she'd spent the morning after the night before in the dorm bathroom. Cate shuddered at the memory. "Let's break open the cassis."

"You are such a lush. Most people would be civilized and have it over ice or something."

"Unless you have a better idea, shut up and hand over the bottle."

He sat back and raised one eyebrow. "As it happens, I do have a better idea."

"If it involves anything but consuming what's in this basket, forget it."

Instead of answering, he opened the little bottle and tilted it against his finger. Then, gently, he brushed his finger against her lower lip, coating it with the sweet liqueur. Cate's first instinct was to lick it off, but curiosity held her still.

Her patience was rewarded when Daniel leaned in and ran his tongue along her lower lip, then kissed her with slow thoroughness. The taste of black currants and the flavor that was uniquely him mingled in a heady brew that went straight to Cate's head.

With Daniel, she never knew what was going to happen. Even something as simple as eating became illuminated with sensual possibility. The fact was that he was more experienced than her, so that in the world of sex, she became the adventurer, the one who explored and discovered. And oddly, that seemed to be just fine with him.

Content to let the moment take them where it would, Cate bit a chocolate in half and put the other half between Daniel's lips. A tiny trickle of caramel escaped and before he could lick it off, she reached up and touched her tongue to the wisp of sweetness at the corner of his mouth.

"Hey now, don't be stealing my caramel."

He selected a Bosc pear, the bronze color of an ancient statue, and sectioned it with the penknife in his pocket.

She'd forgotten he always carried a little knife with him. "That's such a guy thing."

"What? Slicing up fruit?"

"No, having a knife in your pocket all the time. Do

you get separation anxiety at airports when you can't have it on the plane?"

He handed her a slice of pear and wiped the juice off the blade. "No. And it's not a guy thing. It's just practical. I can trim my nails, pick a lock, slice a pear, open a package or whittle something, whenever I want."

"Except for opening a package, I've never been tempted to do any of those things with a knife. So I'm right. It is a guy thing."

"You'd think differently if you'd been in the green room on *Jah-Redd*. One of the techs tie-wrapped a bunch of cable together and then found out they needed it in a couple of minutes for some more lights. You can't undo tie-wraps once they're in place, so they had to cut them."

"I get it," Cate said. "There you were with your trusty pocket knife."

"I have a rep to keep up." He handed her another slice of pear with such serene complacency that Cate began to have second thoughts about her second thoughts.

"I know how important that is to you."

"Do you?" He raised one eyebrow.

"Well, it must be or you wouldn't find so many ways to keep yourself in the spotlight."

"Maybe we should clarify just what kind of rep I meant." His tone had become almost bland, which Cate had the uncomfortable feeling meant she had offended him somehow. And she didn't want to offend him. Not when he was feeding her pears and chocolate in the middle of the morning.

"Maybe we should," she agreed. "You have to admit you are in the public eye a lot. More than your average academic."

"I'm not your average academic. I'm hardly ever on campus. I'm the only prof who puts in expense reports for the worldwide-access coverage on my cell phone."

The most she ever put in for was the odd conference fee and her publication subscriptions. "That's what I mean. Even that has an element of glamour to it."

"It's practical. Cate, why do you see everything I do as some kind of attention-getting scheme?"

Because it is. Because that's the kind of man you are. Isn't it?

If it was, what did that say about her, having a fling with a man like that? In that case, she'd be as bad as any of his arm candy, latching on to him in the hopes that some of his glamour would rub off on her.

Cate shifted uncomfortably and tried to formulate an answer. "Because everything you do seems to attract attention, whether you intend it to or not. How can you be surprised when someone thinks that way?"

"Because I'm a serious scientist." He straightened, and she was forced to straighten up herself or fall over. Cool air flowed between them. "I can't help that my work attracts attention—that it appeals to something in the public psyche. In the end, it's all about the work. The only thing real is what I am in the field."

For heaven's sake, his entire career contradicted him. "Then what on earth possessed you to write that book?" she burst out. "What is a serious archaeologist doing, writing something like that?"

He swallowed the last of the pear and wouldn't meet

her eyes. To her astonishment, ruddy color washed into his face under the tan.

He mumbled something around a gulp of liqueur and she blinked. She couldn't have heard him properly. She must have misunderstood. "What?"

"I said, I didn't write that book."

Cate's jaw hung open for a moment before she collected herself enough to speak. "Who did?"

He shrugged, as uncomfortable as she'd ever seen him since the day the class had laughed at him over the shark's tooth. "Some ghostwriter my publisher dug up."

Well, if this wasn't newsworthy, she didn't know what was. "Do you mean to tell me that that book on the *New York Times* nonfiction bestseller list wasn't written by you at all? That some other person wrote it?"

"Yep." He drained the little bottle and opened the Glenlivet. "He spent a week in the field with me, then another week taping interviews with me in Long Beach, and then he took all my assistant's scrapbooks back to Colorado with him and wrote the book. I'm surprised you couldn't tell it wasn't me."

"Daniel, until now I hadn't seen you in eight years. How was I supposed to know what your writing was like?"

"It's not a bad piece of work, really, but you're right, it definitely has a Hollywood tone to it. Not surprising when you know the last thing the guy did was a biography of Errol Flynn. Also put out by my publisher, if you'll forgive the expression."

"It's none of my business, but you might want to try a university press next time. God knows a dozen of them would jump at the chance." She sat back against the cushions of the couch, and Daniel slid an arm around her shoulders and pulled her closer.

Across the room, cartons of books sat neatly piled on the floor, waiting for the next segment of the tour.

Cate shook her head in disbelief. "Aren't you supposed to have 'as told to' on the cover? So you don't mislead people?"

"It's all about perception. My publisher figured people would expect an archaeologist to be able to write a coherent sentence. Which I can, but not the way the writer did. Hollywood or not, the guy knows how to hook a reader. So they paid him a pile of money and my name went on there instead of his." He squeezed her shoulders. "So are you going to bust me out? Expose me as a fraud?"

"Why should I? It's your story—your life, whether you wrote the words or not. And, again, it's none of my business."

"You sure about that?"

"What do you mean?"

"Only that a serious academic might not want to be seen with a media hound like me."

"That part you bring on yourself. You don't have to go prancing around in front of cameras with models, you know."

"You have to admit, it builds public awareness of what I'm doing."

"Yes, but what kind? The kind that gets you respect, or the kind that gets you tabloid coverage?"

He shrugged and she bit back her frustration. She needed to remember that this was a fling. What he did with himself and his career would be nothing to her once they'd parted ways. It was just her natural inclination— talent, even—to try to help him see that if he wanted public recognition, there were better ways to manage it.

If she'd been the one advising him, now, she would never have recommended a ghostwriter. She'd have gone to a university press, and while it might not have made the nonfiction bestseller list, it would have reaped him the kind of recognition that counted.

The kind of recognition she'd been battling for all her working life. But obviously he wasn't doing these things for that kind of respect. He was doing it for the publicity it would bring. For the funding. For the glory.

She laid her head on his shoulder and he pulled her closer. If he had been different—or if she had—they might have ended up together long ago. Cate could hardly imagine having Daniel next to her every single day for the rest of her life. A sleepy Sunday morning, with orange juice instead of amaretto, and the *New York Times* all over the floor, with or without his book in the review section.

But there was no point in thinking that way. Despite the mind-bending sex and their common love of antiquities and chocolate caramels, their views were too different. In her weaker moments she might not want it that way, but there was no getting around it.

With her other love affairs, there was always some obstacle she couldn't get over as well. Robert, with whom her friend Julia had set her up on a blind date, had stuck around for a couple of months, but since he was a stockbroker, he always had somewhere to be and someone to see. Byron, the visiting lecturer, had lasted a little longer—a whole academic year. She'd actually had hopes for him, but before he'd gone back to England he'd told her very kindly that if she wanted to sustain something long-term, she should consider being a little more feminine. After she'd gotten over her hurt and astonishment, she'd heard one day through the grapevine that he'd had an operation and was now to be addressed in correspondence as Bryony, with the honorific of Ms.

And Charles Morton, the acting head of anthropology? Cate closed her eyes and breathed in the warm scent of Daniel's skin to override the memory. Every sexual encounter they'd had was tainted and abbreviated by his guilt over cheating on his wife—who had divorced him the year before. When he'd taken a position at Northwestern, it was to move to the town she lived in, and the last Cate heard, they were getting remarried.

No, considering her romantic history, and despite his love of the limelight, when you saw him just as a talented man, Daniel was the pick of the bunch.

What a pity he could only be a fling.

11

BOTH OF THEM FELL ASLEEP on the couch, and when Daniel woke, one side of him was warm where Cate lay against him, and the other chilled. This close to the ocean, in late spring, buildings cooled quickly once the sun traveled past the windows. He moved a little, hoping to feel the blood coming back into the arm on which Cate leaned, and she murmured and slid back into sleep. Her blondish brown hair streamed over his skin, where the strands caught in the curly hairs on his chest.

He loved how she'd made love last night—on the beach, under the tree, wherever he'd suggested it. What a long way she'd come. They had been so immature in Mexico. He'd been the more experienced, but as far as being ready for a relationship, he'd been no more capable of that than of jumping from one of the four-hundred-foot sandstone cliffs and surviving. Because what had making love been about, back then? Enjoying the shape and sensations of a young woman's body, enjoying what they did for him.

Orgasm, in other words. He made love for the payoff, and while that might have satisfied many a woman, even at twenty Cate had known with some primal instinct that it wouldn't satisfy her.

He had to give her credit for leaving instead of taking second best from him. But what about now? Was he still that same guy, enjoying the chase and appreciating the prey, but leaving the moment he'd captured what he wanted?

Not a chance. He'd been missing Cate for eight years, keeping her picture in his briefcase to remind himself that there was someone out there who had substance and meaning. Keeping him from making stupid mistakes. She'd influenced him even when she'd vanished from his life and picked up her own with no sign that she felt the same way about him.

But here he was, a little older and hopefully a lot smarter about what he wanted out of life. The short-term girl didn't satisfy him anymore, and neither did coming home to an empty condo that still, after three years, smelt faintly of paint and echoed because he never stuck around long enough to put proper furniture in it. Even if he had any, he couldn't guarantee he'd be around to sit on it for more than five minutes.

He entertained a brief fantasy of coming home to Cate, of rolling on a couch that belonged to them both and eating food they'd both chosen and cooked instead of takeout from the list of restaurants programmed into his cell phone.

Well, if she feels the same way, why does this have to be a fantasy? Why can't it be real?

For one thing, Cate lived in New York and he lived in Long Beach. Both of them had successful careers and friends and things they loved to do. If he and Cate were together, he'd have to cut back the expeditions and concentrate on teaching a little more seriously than he had up until now. One of them might have to think about relocating. He had no problem with New York, so it would likely be him.

It's only been a couple of days. Don't start choosing the china patterns yet.

The only kinds of pottery he had been any good at until now were made by ancient civilizations, but that didn't mean he couldn't update his skills. What he needed to do was romance her. Woo her. Let her know that he was different, she was different, and together they might do things differently this time. So she had a little problem with the visibility of his career. They could work it out. And if they couldn't, then so be it. At least he would have gone for what he wanted.

The good thing was that what Daniel Burke wanted was usually what he got.

Cate lifted her chin to peer at the clock in the kitchenette. "Does that really say one-thirty?"

"Probably." He didn't care what time it was. There was nowhere he had to be today, and no one he'd rather be nowhere with than Cate.

"But we missed the whole morning program! Not to mention the closing lunch."

"Is that a problem?"

"Yes, it's a problem. I wanted to hear Dr. Manov talk about female symbology in Middle Eastern art. I guess I'll have to buy the tape."

Grinning, he hauled her up and wrapped his arms

around her. "I'd love to talk about female symbology with you. Would you like to start with the vulva or the breasts?"

"Neither. My leopard cults have made me interested in dentition. How do you feel about the toothed orifice?"

"The what?"

She lay against him, smug and warm, her arms looped around his neck. "Isn't that what men fear the most? A woman's mouth?"

"They have a good reason to fear it. More than one good reason. Me, I just want to kiss yours. It's not very scary right now." He dipped his head and her lips parted with unhurried enjoyment under his. When he lifted his head again, he added, "Just don't wear your fanged bunny slippers around me. Those make me really nervous."

Her face lit with laughter and a certain feminine knowledge that might have taunted a less secure guy. He traced the shape of one breast through her T-shirt with a finger.

"Since the conference is over, what do you think we should do? Besides making love until the earth moves again."

"Checkout is three o'clock."

"And why am I not surprised that you know this?"

"Daniel, honestly, how do you get yourself to your digs and appearances and presentations? A person has to pay attention to these kinds of details."

"My people know them. That's what I pay them for."

She sat up, and he took a moment to admire the purity of the line from chin to collarbone. "You do not have 'people.'"

"No, I don't," he confessed. "Stacy Mills calls my cell phone constantly to make sure I'm where I'm supposed to be on this tour. I always know, but she figures I'm going to get distracted and forget to show up at some talk she has scheduled for five hundred people."

She relaxed a little, and he propped his head on his hand to watch her.

"So where do you have to be next?" she asked.

"San Francisco. By Wednesday. I'm supposed to be on some TV segment in Oakland that night, do a talk and a book signing the next day at the Museum of Art, and have dinner with some big shot. I forget who. A Rockefeller, I think."

"My word."

Her skin was so soft he couldn't resist touching it, just a short trip down her jawline from ear to chin. "But until Wednesday night I have absolutely nothing on the agenda. Except probably a dozen calls from Stacy. Other than that, I can get there as fast or as slow as I choose."

"Really." She waited.

"How soon do you have to go back?"

She shrugged. "It's reading week. No official duties until exams start next Monday. I can play hooky until Wednesday, but I have to be back for a staff meeting on Thursday."

"So what do you say we throw your bag in the back seat and head on up the coast? Get a bed-and-breakfast in Santa Rita, browse the antique shops in Los Gatos, and generally goof off before we have to go back to work?"

In a couple of days, who knew what might happen? Cate wasn't a wishy-washy woman. She was smart and talented and knew what she wanted. A few days might not seem like much, but entire lives could change in that time.

After all, between one day and the next, he and his team had discovered the Temecula Treasure, and his whole life had taken a ninety-degree turn and headed off in a direction he would never have imagined. Maybe these few days stolen out of time would have the same result.

And if they didn't, they would not have lost anything. If something wasn't meant to grow between Cate and himself, then fine. But if it was, Daniel wanted to give it every chance.

Who knew what treasure he'd bring home from this trip?

CATE ACTUALLY FELT HER LEGS tremble as she rolled her discreet black carry-on across the lawn, under those prickly oaks from which her feet were not yet recovered, toward the parking lot where Daniel's vintage Camaro was parked.

Her muscles, which were prepared for everything from climbing the stairs on campus to scaling rocks in Colorado, had been totally unprepared for sex. In fact, there were a whole set of muscles in her inner thighs that felt like a bunch of drunken church ladies, wobbling and hooting instead of getting on with the job.

She hoped that, like any muscle, they'd toughen up a bit with regular workouts. Because for the next three days—Sunday evening to Wednesday afternoon—she planned to exercise them at every possible opportunity.

If she was only to have Daniel for three days, she'd make sure they were three days he wasn't going to forget in a hurry. In fact, maybe they'd make him think the next time he jumped in front of a camera to sell his talent short.

But thinking about cameras took a little of the shine off the afternoon, so Cate shoved them off the stage of her imagination. Instead, she tied her sweater around her shoulders and waved as Daniel strode toward her, his duffel slung over one shoulder and Stacy Mills running beside him, cell phone to one ear and a stream of what sounded like instructions floating over the lot as they crossed it.

"Daniel, please remember you need to be in the KTVU studios in Oakland by five o'clock Wednesday afternoon for the taping, so make sure you dress appropriately. No white shirts, no busy patterns on the tie—what? Oh, yes, sorry, I'll hold. I swear, the museum needs more than one person on the switchboard. I'll have the copies of your books shipped from here to the museum, and you'll need to be there at 11:00 a.m. on Thursday. Daniel, are you listening?"

"Have a good trip north, Stacy. And thanks for all your hard work." He tossed the duffel in the back seat next to Cate's suitcase, slid behind the wheel and fired up the engine. Its throaty roar totally drowned out poor Stacy, who stood with her mouth still moving while he slung gravel around the tight turn onto the drive.

The breeze blew in Cate's face as they turned north onto the highway a moment later, and she relaxed as the sun poured down, glinting in a million chips of light on the ocean far below.

"That poor girl is just trying to do her job." She glanced at Daniel and pulled a flying strand of hair out of her eyes.

"And she does it well. I think she thinks I'm one of

her absentminded fiction people, though. If I can put together an expedition to the Turkish desert, I can certainly get myself to a TV studio four or five hours away." He glanced at her and grinned. "Eventually."

That grin held the promise of sin and sensuality, and Cate felt a rush of desire that tightened her thighs and made her clit quiver in response. She pushed all unpleasant thoughts out of her mind and sat back on the old-fashioned bench seat of the Camaro as he navigated the looping curves of the highway, astounded that a simple movement of his face could trigger such a response in her own body. It was as if they were two parts of a whole, and his thoughts produced her reactions, instantly.

Wow.

She was discovering all kinds of interesting things about her sexuality—and that was only after twenty-four hours. If she kept her focus on simply enjoying herself, imagine what she'd know in three days.

"Daniel," she said, "do men actually prefer oral or vaginal sex? Performing it, I mean. On a woman."

His grin got wider and then he threw back his head and laughed.

"What's so funny?" She hadn't said anything remotely amusing. She really wanted to know—and she didn't have an Internet connection or a library handy with which to find out.

"You." He reached over and squeezed her knee. "You sounded as if you were posing the question to your first-year students."

"I was posing it to someone who might be expected

to know. Though I suppose you could say that of any first-year student."

"To be honest, I don't know about men in general—or rather, locker-room conversations can't be trusted. I only know for sure about me."

Again, her body did that little internal shimmy of anticipation. "Tell me."

"I like sex in all its wonderful variations, but I've discovered that there's a certain pleasure my partner gets when I give her oral sex that she doesn't get any other way. And since pleasing my partner is becoming more important to me, I'd have to say I prefer that."

No one had ever done that for Cate. Somehow she felt deprived, as if millions of happy women knew something she didn't. She'd masturbated, of course, but she was quite sure it wouldn't feel the same.

"Why do you ask?"

She should have thought about this. Now she'd have to confess that there was yet one more thing about sex about which she was ignorant. But trying to hide something like that from Daniel would be ludicrous—especially when chances were probably one hundred percent that he'd be happy to bring her up to date.

"I was just curious," she said at last.

"I like that in a woman." He kept his eyes on the road. "Cate."

"Yes?"

"Has no one ever gone down on you?"

"Is that surprising?" she said a little stiffly.

"I don't know." Instead of merely squeezing her knee, he ran his free hand under her skirt and as far up her bare leg as the taut fabric would allow. "But if you want to, we can correct this deficit in your experience as soon as I can find a place to pull over."

"Daniel Burke, you will not!"

"Why not?"

"Because—because—"

She had to think of a reason, and quick. He would never back down from a challenge like that. Not to mention the fact that her sexual education had clearly become a personal mission for him.

"Because we'll be arrested for indecent exposure!"

"Not if we're discreet." He scanned the roadsides, but there was nothing on the left but a sheer drop of a hundred feet to the ocean, and on the right empty reaches of low-lying scrub that offered no cover at all.

Good grief. She sounded like a military strategist. One who couldn't help staring in fascination at what was happening behind the button fly of his jeans.

"It is completely impossible for me to be discreet when I'm having an orgasm, and you know it," she said a little breathlessly.

Her face flushed with the forbidden excitement of it, and her blood was flying through her veins, each red cell rushing to be the first into her swollen femininity.

He laughed again. "And I'm glad to hear it. Look. Up ahead. It's perfect."

On the left, the road widened for about twenty feet, and the department of highways had planted two huge boulders there, presumably so people wouldn't take a suicide dive off the edge. Spinning the wheel, Daniel backed the Camaro between the boulders with just enough room for the door to open on her side. He hoisted himself straight up and into the back seat, then hopped out on the passenger side and opened her door.

"See?" he said, kneeling on the ground. "No one can see a thing."

Sure enough, the open door shielded him from the view of anyone on the road, and behind there was nothing but the wide sky and the wash of the waves far below. For a woman who craved space and the freedom of open air, to be set free and flying on an orgasm in such a spot was perfect.

Once you got past the whole sex-in-a-public-place part.

"Lie down, Cate," Daniel said. He knelt in the dust and ran his hand up under her skirt a second time. His dark eyes were nearly black with passion and anticipation, triggering an answering jolt of need from her treacherous body. "Let me do this for you."

She simply must have it. There was no use telling herself they needed to wait until they had a motel room and a bed and all the trappings of civilization. On the side of a highway, on the edge of the continent—if she didn't let him have his way, she would regret it forever.

This was a fling. That was the whole meaning of *fling*, wasn't it? To do something with wild abandon and unexpected force. That wasn't to say that she couldn't still control its direction—she had pretty good aim. She'd thought this out and decided on her course of action, so doing this with Daniel was the next logical step.

If a fling could be said to be logical.

One flung caution to the winds, so that was exactly what she was going to do.

12

DANIEL TUGGED GENTLY on her knee and turned her toward him on the seat.

"Should I take my sandals off?" Cate asked.

"Leave them on. I like 'em. The skirt has to go, though."

She undid the button and zipper and slid out of it, then tossed it in the back.

"That's right," he breathed, running his hands down her thighs and calves. His hands were so warm, and her skin felt so shivery and alive. "You have the greatest legs in the western world." He positioned himself between her legs and licked the sensitive skin on the inside of one knee.

It felt delicious.

It felt even better on her inner thigh, where the cool air off the ocean contrasted with the hot slickness of his tongue and his breath against her skin.

Her spine seemed to melt and the sky spun a little as she relaxed back onto the bench seat. Chevrolet had done women everywhere a disservice when it had begun to put bucket seats into its cars, she thought in some faraway corner of her brain as Daniel hooked his fingers in her lace panties and pulled them over her hips, thighs, and finally off altogether. With a flick of his wrist, he fired them past her and they draped themselves on the stick shift.

He bent to the work of torturing her again. She stopped listening for the hum of an approaching car and instead found her concentration narrowing to that glorious inch or so of Daniel's mouth as it traveled inexorably yet with excruciating slowness up her thigh. His tongue swirled on her skin. His teeth nibbled gently. And all the while the anticipation built until her entire body silently begged him to hurry. Even her fingers and toes were making tiny, convulsive movements, as if beckoning him in. Come on…come on….

He paused at the very apex of her thighs and she nearly screamed. "Are you ready for me, Cate?"

She'd never been so ready for anything in her life. Not to mention the fact that any of the cars driving past might decide to stop and take in the scenery at any moment. The urgent need to have what she wanted before someone came along to deprive her of it gave an added dimension to the force of her desire.

"Yes! Please…you're killing me."

He wasted no more time. She felt his gentle fingers exploring, parting, smoothing the way. And then…oh, then…he stroked her first with one long movement of his tongue and she came right up off the seat with a cry.

"Easy. Easy, sweetheart." Warm hands on her inner thighs pressed her back down, opening her wider for the sensual attack of his mouth. His tongue was hot and slick and absolutely unlike anything she'd ever experienced. She couldn't control him—couldn't direct him to do anything because this was completely new. He traveled with slow precision over each of her folds, culminating at the apex with her clit, where he settled down to serious business.

It was excitement, it was pleasure, it was sensation in its purest form—and she adored it. Sparks seemed to fly in the deepest parts of her belly, and she felt the pleasure peak and wane, then peak again, stronger. Then she felt her orgasm coming with the force of a tidal wave and she called out, "Daniel!" as it crashed over her and still he didn't stop and she was writhing under his mouth, screaming his name and it was coming again under his relentless tongue, harder and faster this time and she grabbed the dashboard with one hand and the back of the seat with the other and let it take her, pummel her, throw her up into the endless air and set her down, as gently as a feather lands on the water....

DANIEL LIFTED HIS HEAD.

Cate lay helplessly on the seat, her head thrown back, gasping and laughing at once, with tears on her lashes. The flavor of her, creamy and musky and utterly unique to this remarkable woman, lay on his skin and his tongue like a fine wine.

He knelt on the outer edge of the seat and propped himself over her. "Cate?"

She could hardly speak. "My God, Daniel. That was...wonderful. Oh, my God."

What kind of jokers had she dated who had never given her this pleasure before? Not that he minded. He was damned happy that it was him enjoying this moment, giving her all he had and sharing a slightly wicked taste for exhibitionism that he never would have suspected lay under those tidy white blouses and slim, proper skirts.

The need to tear his jeans off and plunge into her while she was gasping and wet and sprawled open for the taking swamped him, but he controlled it with a formidable exercise of will.

She sat up, and he relaxed into a comfortable kneeling position on a handy tussock of grass. "What about you?" Her eyes were soft and hungry and satisfied, all at once, and her mouth had that slack sensuality that begged a kiss.

He pulled her head down and gave it to her. "I can keep."

"I don't think so." She reached down and fondled him through his jeans, and the touch of her fingers sent a rocket blast of sensation through his engorged erection, rocking him back. "Feel how hard you are."

"I do, don't worry. Can you blame me? That was amazing."

"You are amazing." She kissed him this time, her hair falling forward and tenting their faces for a few brief moments before the breeze caught it and blew it back. "I never had any idea. I'd read about it, of course, but never thought it would be like that. Thank you."

Her eyes were still wet. Had he ever made a woman laugh and cry at the same time? Somehow, he didn't think so. If he had given her a gift, then she had given him one, too—the knowledge that what they'd done had shaken her and perhaps even touched her in some deep place inside.

It was a start. He was the kind of guy who enjoyed the journey as well as the destination. The process as well as the prize. With Cate, the journey was promising to be exciting and full of prizes along the way.

"Daniel, you have to let me satisfy you," Cate insisted. She looked so cute in her summer tank top with nothing on but sandals south of its hem.

He leaned over and picked her undies off the gear shift. "You will," he promised. "But for now, let's not push our luck."

It wasn't exactly easy to move as he hopped back into the driver's seat, as aroused as he was, but he managed it. Which turned out to be a lucky thing, because a second later, a California Highway Patrol vehicle came around the curve and signaled a left turn.

"Daniel!" Cate yelped. "He's coming over here!" She tried to yank her underwear on, but it twisted into a delicate little rope around one ankle. With a frantic glance at the car coming to a stop ten feet away, she grabbed her skirt, but there was no time to pull it on and do it up. She laid the skirt flat on her lap and casually leaned back, pressing her elbows against the side seams so they would lie flat against her thighs.

The patrolman got out of the car. "Having problems here, folks?"

Cate made a sound something like a squeak.

Daniel felt himself deflating so fast his jeans had become almost comfortable again. "Not at all. We were just taking in the view."

The cop glanced at the car, parked backward, and at the two of them, facing the scrubby slope opposite.

"Uh-huh. Just so you know, it's not safe to park there. I'll need to ask you to move along. Wouldn't want you going down."

Another muffled sound came from the passenger seat and Daniel covered it up smoothly. "We were just doing that. Have a good day, Officer."

He started the engine and was about to put the car in gear when the officer laid his hand on the hood. Cate scooted a little farther into the corner of the seat.

"Say, you look familiar. Aren't you that explorer guy? The one who was on *Jah-Redd* last week?"

Daniel let out the clutch and rolled forward, so that the door was no longer pinned against the rock. He stretched out a hand. "Daniel Burke. And yes, you're correct."

The officer grinned. "I bought your book for my dad. Damn. I wish I had it with me so you could sign it."

"Give me your card and I'll send a signed bookplate to your office. How's that?"

"Thanks." The cop dug a card out of his pocket and handed it over. "Have a pleasant day, Mr. Burke."

"You, too."

Daniel pressed the accelerator and turned onto the highway, keeping his speed to the limit in case the cop decided to give them a police escort all the way up the coast. He glanced at Cate, who still had her elbows pressed into her sides and was gasping for breath.

"Good thing you didn't talk me into anything naughty back there. The only autograph he would have had is my signature on a ticket for public indecency."

Then he realized she wasn't hyperventilating at all. She was whooping with laughter as she pulled her skirt on properly, then shook out her underwear and pulled it on as well.

"Hey, it's not funny," he complained.

Cate wiped tears from one cheek with the flat of her hand. "All through high school I never got the chance to neck with a boy in the back of a car and get busted by the local cop," she said, buckling her seat belt. "And here I am, twenty-eight and in broad daylight, when it finally happens."

"We're damn lucky he took an extra minute at lunch today. Otherwise he'd have caught me...er, going down. And not over any cliffs, either."

She leaned over and kissed him on the cheek. "And here I thought this conference was going to be so dull. I can't wait to see what happens next."

As soon as he found them a place to stay, he was going to take great pleasure in showing her.

The Egret Inn, which they discovered an hour later just south of the town of Santa Rita, was a huge, spreading Victorian mansion painted white with gray gingerbread and green trim. It was situated on the high ground between the sand dunes that fronted the ocean on the west and a wetland bird sanctuary to the east.

"Look at the egrets!" Cate dropped her bag on the ground next to the car and jogged to the edge of the parking lot, where the slow-moving water was nearly white with a flock of the stork-like birds. Daniel grinned at her delight.

"I forgot how you are about things with wings."

She glanced over her shoulder at him, her hair blowing across her face in the breeze, her eyes lit with enjoyment. "They're lovely." She pointed out into the marsh. "And there are Canada geese here still. I thought they would have migrated north by now."

"Maybe they're California geese. Too laid-back to travel. All they need are some shades and a margarita."

"Ooh, I could use one of those." She collected her abandoned bag, and in a few minutes they were registered and Daniel was holding open the door of their room so she could roll her bag in.

"This is nice."

The Egret Inn was evidently meant for the honeymoon market. The bed was comfortable and wide, the cushions on the window seats were thick, and the plank floor was covered by a rug into which his feet sank. Picture windows looked out onto the bird sanctuary, and he wondered if that was a mistake. He didn't want Cate on the window seat, spending all her time watching birds who didn't know when it was time to go home. He wanted her on the bed, on the rug, in the shower—anywhere but on the window seat.

Call him a selfish bastard, but he had a plan, here, and no bird was going to get in the way.

Naturally Cate headed straight for the window seat.

"Look, there's a raised boardwalk trail through the sanctuary." She pointed. "You know, like they do in the Everglades. Let's go, Daniel, before we lose the light."

So much for the bed, the rug and the shower. "How long are you going to make me suffer, woman?"

She left the window and came into his arms. "Poor baby. Are you suffering?"

That was better. "Well, maybe not suffering. That cop

scared my libido into the next county. It's on its way back, though, in case you were worried."

She grinned up at him and gave him a kiss. "That's the last thing I'm worried about. Humor me and come for a walk."

"At least it's not a mall or something. I should be grateful."

"I save malls for special people like girlfriends. They're wasted on a guy."

He'd been in wetland before—up to his hips in malaria-ridden, brackish water, fighting snakes and jungle insects on his way to the discovery of the Temecula Treasure. This one was a walk in the park—literally. The boardwalk wound through the sanctuary a couple of feet above the water, allowing things to swim around practically under their feet. By the time they were back on solid ground again an hour later, the bird geek at his side had identified no fewer than seventeen species.

He'd thought there were only five or so, but she'd pointed out his error in great detail. Some day he'd take her on one of those eco-tours to the Galapagos or something and really knock her socks off.

But in a way it was kind of endearing. At least when she got that beady look in her eye, it was over some kind of goldfinch, and not something gold. As in Tiffany or Harry Winston. He should count his blessings.

Cate went to unpack her suitcase and stopped next to the bed. She picked up the long-stemmed yellow rose that lay on the pillow. "Daniel, you think of everything." She breathed deeply of the scent. "Thank you."

He could have sworn that hadn't been there when

they'd left. "For the price of this room, I'd have expected a whole bouquet. But it is a nice touch."

She looked at him quizzically, brushing the bright petals of the rose against her chin. "You mean you didn't arrange to have them bring it? The inn does this kind of thing for its guests?"

He shrugged. "Guess so. You'll find I'm more likely to bring you—"

"I know—"

"Rocks as big as diamonds," she chorused with him. She filled the ice bucket with water and put the rose in it. "I'm starving. Let's go see what the restaurant downstairs is like."

He came up behind her and took her in his arms. "I just spent forty-five minutes with a bunch of birds for you, and now you want to go eat?" he teased. He was only half kidding. Even the scent of her hair and warm skin could turn him on, and he was more than ready to put dinner off until dark—or beyond. "We still need to even the score."

She gave him a skeptical look and leaned into him. "Oh, come on. It can't have been that long since your last starlet. You can last another two hours."

A week ago he would have laughed and made a joke about it. Now the needlelike lance of pain surprised him. He couldn't blame her for saying it—he hadn't hidden his social life from the world. And they'd only been together for a couple of days. They were still getting to know each other. But when you were trying to convince a woman to think about you in a more flattering light, having your past tossed in your face got old in a hurry.

Turning her around to face him, he said, "Just how long do you think that has been?" Her gaze searched his, and she seemed to realize that he wasn't joking anymore. "Let me tell you," he answered for her. "The last time I made love to a woman was on March third, with Dulcie Cavanaugh, the *National Geographic* photographer. More than two months ago. The night before she told me she was taking an assignment to Antarctica and wouldn't be coming back to L.A."

"I don't remember reading about Dulcie Cavanaugh," Cate said faintly.

"The ones I really like don't get into the papers," he told her. "The ones you read about are usually studio setups or publicity stunts or whatever."

"I have no idea how that world works."

"Good. Let's keep it that way."

She leaned on him and looped her arms around his waist. "Were you hurt when Dulcie left?"

"A little." He thought of the big-boned redhead with the boisterous laugh. "She was smart and well traveled. We met at a book gig and my publisher introduced us. I think he was hoping to get one of her photos for my next cover." He looked into her eyes. "Which will be on a book I write myself. But if that was a roundabout way of asking whether I loved her, the answer is also yes, a little."

Her weight on his chest got a little heavier, as though she had sagged, and then she adjusted her stance.

"And now?"

"Every relationship we have changes us, Cate. But that doesn't mean a change for the worse."

"That's comforting." Her voice held a smile.

"As far as you and I are concerned, every minute is better than the last one." He paused. "Well, except for the near miss with that seagull outside just now. Can't say that was one of my more romantic moments."

As he had hoped, Cate laughed and the mood broke. She gazed over his shoulder at the window. "It's twilight. Come on, let's have dinner and then go over the dunes and walk on the beach afterward."

"Do you always have this much energy?" he complained as he released her and went to find a fresh shirt.

She shot him a wicked grin as she opened her suitcase. "Oh, yes. I have every intention of wearing you out when we get back."

"In that case, let's go."

13

THE INN'S DINING ROOM specialized in fresh catches from the marina down the way. Cate chose deep-fried calamari with the knowledge that a walk on the beach and a night making love would erase every single carb from her system.

She could hardly wait.

Daniel tucked into his halibut and chips like a man who was used to eating while he could, in case there was no food around the next bend in the road. Why, she wondered as she watched him, had she avoided him for eight years? The more time she spent with him, the more she realized that the open-hearted boy with the devilishly charming smile was still alive and well. She'd depended too much on media perceptions of him—of other people's opinions, not her own. That was all very well in academia, where other people's opinions formed the bedrock on which theses were built, but it didn't work in relationships. There, a hands-on approach was required.

She had avoided that in her professional life, too, hadn't she? She'd spend hours in her office on a paper instead of getting out in the field and making her own discoveries. Just what had she been afraid of? There was nothing wrong with theory, but there came a point when you had to have fresh data to back it up.

With Daniel, getting that data was going to be a pleasure.

As she savored her crème brûlée some time later, Daniel sipped a glass of port. He saluted her with it over the low-burning candle on the table.

She smiled back, taking a moment to appreciate his dark eyes and the way they seemed to communicate every emotion. Such a difference between him and someone like Charles, who was so locked in his own guilt that his gray eyes had been blank with horror at himself half the time.

No wonder she hadn't been orgasmic with that guy. Sex—or the lack of it—had been all about him.

They charged the meal to their room and strolled outside, where the fog was beginning to come in. "Sure you want that walk on the beach?" Daniel asked as they crossed the wooden planks of the veranda. "Could be pretty cool, and we won't be able to see much."

"No one would be able to see us," she suggested, looking on the bright side.

He laughed. "I'm okay with making love to you at sixty or seventy degrees, but anything below that? I'm thinking goose bumps aren't all that romantic."

He had a point. And it was a shame to pay all that money for a bed and use cold sand instead. "In the morning, then. I want my walk on the beach before I go back to New York."

"That's a deal."

Hand in hand, they climbed the stairs to their room. As he held the door for her, Cate felt the heat coming off his body. Her own temperature was rising in anticipation of the night—helped along by the fact that every time he brushed her skin in passing, or she caught a whiff of his cologne, she felt that jolt deep inside.

Did every woman feel this way about one particular man in her life? And what if, once their fling was over, she never felt like this again? What a depressing thought—to go through life with a partner you loved but without this spicy zing of awareness every time you saw or touched him.

Oh, grow up, Cate.

Relationships weren't about the zing, or about the fling. They were about time and respect and commitment. She might have had two out of three at one time or another, but the commitment—and, face it, the zing—were definitely missing.

Just what did a girl have to do to get commitment *and* zing?

"Man, that rose has some scent." Daniel closed the door and crossed the room to open a window. "How can one flower stink up a room so much?"

"That's not a rose." Cate sniffed and identified the perfume right away. She had not spent hours in the cosmetics department of Bloomie's for nothing. "That's Allure, by Chanel."

"Did you break your bottle? I didn't think the Camaro's ride was that rough."

"I didn't bring anything on this trip. The conference was scent-free, remember?"

Daniel made a face. "Must have missed that memo, too. God, where is it coming from? It reeks in here."

The scent got stronger and less pleasant the closer Cate came to the bed. "Daniel, it's the sheets." She touched the pillow and the neatly turned-down coverlet. "They're soaked with it."

"What the hell...? If this is service, I draw the line." He picked up the phone and punched a button. "Front desk? Yeah, this is Daniel Burke in number seven. Does your turndown service usually include perfume? Perfume. You know, stinky stuff poured all over my sheets? No? I didn't think so. You want to send housekeeping up here? Or better yet, how about you give us another room before we die of Allure poisoning." He listened for a moment. "Okay, full house, I get that. But I still want the bed changed out. Right. Thanks."

He put the phone down. "They're sending someone up."

Cate was already stripping the bed. In a few seconds she'd bundled sheets, pillowcases, blankets and even the mattress cover out into the hallway and opened every window she could find. The cool, fog-laden air drifted in and began to clear the miasma of perfume.

"Gack," she said, fanning the air in front of her face. "And to think I used to like that stuff."

"What I'd like to know is, who got in here and dumped it on our bed? We're lucky they didn't get into our luggage."

"Or did they?"

Cate ran to her suitcase and flipped it open. With a breath of relief tainted by the fading scent of perfume, she ran a hand over her clothes. Nothing seemed to have been disturbed, and nothing was wet. "Daniel, is your stuff okay?"

He looked up from his examination of his duffel. "Seems to be. Maybe one of the maids had an accident."

She straightened and frowned at the bare mattress. "A maid wouldn't bring a bottle of perfume into a room, much less accidentally spill a couple of ounces on the bed. A couple of drops, I could see, but that stuff costs a fortune."

"So what are you saying?" He dropped the duffel and leaned a hip on the table. "We have a perfume vandal with expensive taste?"

"Does anyone know you're here?" she asked by way of answer. He shook his head. "Not even Stacy Mills?"

"Nope. It's none of her business what I do between gigs. Her job is making sure I get to them. Besides, she doesn't wear this. What you said. Allure."

"An expert in perfumes, too, are we?" She wasn't jealous that he knew what kind of scent his publicist wore. Some men paid attention to that kind of detail. That was all.

"No, but believe me, after this I'm going to be." She'd already opened the window as wide as it would go, but he lifted the old-fashioned sash again, as if to emphasize his point. "Can we breathe yet?"

A knock at the door heralded the arrival of the maid and the housekeeping cart.

"I'm so sorry about this, Mr. Burke, Ms. Wells," she said breathlessly as she whipped out new sheets and slapped them into place with a skill Cate could only stand back and admire. "I can't explain what happened. My goodness, that stuff is strong, isn't it?"

The manager was hot on her heels. "Please accept the inn's apologies for this and be assured we'll be talking to everyone on our staff." He shook Daniel's hand and then Cate's. "I don't understand what could have happened, either, but we'll get to the bottom of it."

"It may not have been the staff at all," Cate said. "Miss, did you see anyone in the vicinity of our room while we were at dinner?"

The maid smoothed the comforter and gave the pillows a final fluff. "No, ma'am. I was doing the beds in number four for a late arrival and didn't see anyone."

"Don't be too hard on the staff, Mr. Moreno," Daniel said to the manager. "I'm sure it was just an accident, with no real harm done. It wasn't as if it was battery acid or something."

"What about this?" Cate indicated the rose in the ice bucket. "Did the hotel provide this, by any chance? We found it on the pillow when we arrived."

"No, Ms. Wells. Even if the hotel did provide such a thing for its guests, I would not put a yellow rose in the room of a couple."

"Why not?" Daniel wanted to know.

"The yellow rose signifies jealousy," the older man said. "A very unlucky thing, would you not agree?"

Indeed, Cate thought as the manager and the maid took their leave, both apologizing at once. It was more than a little disconcerting to know that someone had been in their room not once, but twice. She never gave housekeeping a thought when she stayed in hotels, but this was different. Someone had come in here with the deliberate intent to make their presence—and their jealousy?—known. But to whom? Herself? No, no one cared about her.

But Daniel, now, that was a potsherd of a different color. They'd already had an uninvited guest. Why couldn't they have another one?

"Daniel, did that girl who came to your cottage last night wear Allure?" she asked.

He turned from the window, where he had been doing some more deep breathing. "I have no idea."

"Maybe she followed us here."

"I doubt it. There's a big difference between knocking on the door like a normal person and getting into a locked hotel room like a burglar. Particularly one on the second floor."

"Is there? It's not like these have key-card entries. They're just standard bolts like I have at home. And I can get into mine with a credit card."

"In that case I hope you have a chain on your door."

"But my point is—"

He crossed the room and took her into his arms. "I see your point. But I still think it was an accident. And even if it wasn't, there was no harm done. This is a pretty benign vandal."

"That's just what I mean." She stepped away a little so she could think without getting distracted by things like the solidity of his thighs and how wonderful his hands felt as they slid over her back. "I'm betting it's a woman, not just because of the perfume, but because it does seem benign. She could have dumped it in our clothes or in the furniture, but she chose the sheets."

"Okay, I'll play. Why?"

"Two reasons. You're the symbologist. Perfume plus bed equals…?"

"Um, 'I want to give you nightmares about this smell for the rest of your life'?"

Cate rolled her eyes. "No, silly. 'I want to make sure you remember me while you're making love with someone else in this bed.'"

Daniel laughed. "Come on, Cate. Be serious."

"I am serious. Which leads me to the second reason I think it's a woman. She poured it on the sheets, which can be washed. She makes her point in an unmistakable fashion, but it doesn't really hurt or damage anything. It's easy to clean up. That seems very female to me. Considerate, even, in a twisted way. And add to that the yellow rose, which just emphasizes my point."

Daniel didn't laugh this time, but his grin stretched a little wider. "You, my darling, have been watching way too much *CSI* on television."

"I have not." Okay, so the charming grin wasn't quite so charming when he was using it to discount a perfectly rational theory. "I think you should ask the manager to show you the guest registry. You might see a name on it that you know. Maybe someone carries a grudge."

He started shaking his head somewhere around *registry* and began to laugh again at *grudge*. Cate stopped theorizing and glared at him. "I'm only trying to help."

"I know, and I appreciate it." He sobered a little, but not enough to make the amused smile disappear. "I honestly think it was just a mistake. Someone forgot to put the lid on and spilled, and doesn't want to admit it in case she loses her job. As simple as that."

"There's no need to laugh at my ideas." Cate sounded as stiff and, well, hurt as she felt. "Both of us are just speculating, and just because you're male doesn't give your theories any greater validity than—"

"Whoa!" Daniel took her hand and led her to the bed, where he sat her down. "This is not the archaeology department, Cate. It's not a political arena. It's a bedroom."

"I'm well aware of that." She was also aware that it was impossible to stay angry at Daniel for long. Not with those wonderful expressive eyes locked on her face and those strong hands wrapped around hers. "Excuse me while I put on my bunny slippers."

An expression of horror crossed his face while his eyes danced. "No, no. Please. Not the bunny slippers. You know how they make me feel."

"Say it could very well be a female intruder with an ax to grind and I'll leave them in the suitcase."

He nodded. "It absolutely could. We'll keep our eyes open from here on out. I promise that instead of ogling your breasts I will watch for jealous females following us."

Cate's mood had improved by a hundred percent. Lucky for him, she'd never held a grudge in her life. Lucky for her, he never took anything seriously.

"I wouldn't go that far. I like it when you ogle them. I like it even better when you touch them."

"Well, then," he said softly, "We can't have you disappointed, can we?" He ran one finger from her collarbone down her chest, over the crest of her nipple, to her ribs. Every cell in her body stood to attention. "Turn around."

He ran the zipper of her discreet black sheath down its track and parted the two halves, leaving the bare skin of her back exposed. Cate shivered as his lips traveled slowly over her shoulders, lingering on the nape of her neck. The dress fell down her arms and she slipped out of it.

In only her panties, bra and stockings, she turned to Daniel and began to unbutton his shirt. "You look over-heated," she said sympathetically. "All this excitement."

It was difficult to get the buttons undone while he was removing her bra at the same time, but she managed. And tugging off his shoes, socks and trousers was even more challenging, especially when he seemed to be able to get her panties away from her in a few seconds.

But ah, her reward was waiting for her as he skimmed her stockings down each leg and tossed them over the foot of the bed. His arousal and the focused, intent look in his eyes left no doubt that for him, there was going to be no more waiting. A dozen perfume-wielding intruders couldn't stop him now.

Thank God.

When they were both naked, Cate flung herself on top of him, laughing when he caught her effortlessly and lowered her until they were skin to skin.

"I'm going to pretend that we have weeks and weeks together instead of just two days," she said. "I'm going to block out the whole end of the week and just make tomorrow and Tuesday last forever."

He may have been about to say something, but she lowered her mouth to his and kissed it into silence.

She knew the drill—the whole carpe diem speech. She didn't need to hear it. She was just going to enjoy him for all she was worth and maybe it would warm her from the inside when she went back to New York. Maybe it would change her and she'd attract a different kind of guy. A guy who liked adventure, who had more in his life than school or his ex-wife. A guy like Daniel. Not the Indiana Jones media creation, but the real Daniel—down-to-earth, funny and willing to let her be herself.

She'd find him some day. That was something to look forward to.

Wasn't it?

"Hey. Earth to Cate. No out-of-body experiences when you're lying on top of me."

"Not likely. My brain is full of you." She kissed the corner of his mouth. "My senses are full of you." A kiss on each eyelid. "And shortly my body is going to be, too."

"Promises, promises."

She moved in a sensuous S-curve as she stretched full length on him. "I always keep my promises."

"I believe you promised me something this afternoon."

She was so engorged and ready for him it was a wonder she didn't spontaneously combust. The heat of his body wrapped her in sensuous promise—or maybe it was the heat of his gaze. Or maybe they were one and the same and all she wanted was to bury herself in him.

Or better yet, let him bury himself in her.

Without another word, she lifted herself up on her knees and took the hot length of his erection in both hands. Their gazes locked, and then with a lift of his hips he found that secret place between her legs that seemed to belong to him alone, where he was a perfect fit and every memory of anyone but him was erased. She groaned with satisfaction as the hot, smooth length of him slid inside her. Her mind blanked out and her body took over, meeting his every thrust, her eyes half closed. Still, she was aware of the way he watched her, as if her pleasure increased his own and he wanted to enjoy every nuance of it. Just as she'd been aware of his every breath when they'd made love before, now he focused on her, the sounds she made, making small adjustments so that her pleasure might be increased.

When he lifted his hand and teased her clit with his fingers, adding the sweet, slick friction to the rhythm inside her, the pleasure begin to build. It was like darts of fire, waves of anticipation and need, all rolled into one. The explosion rolled through her, centered on his finger like the eye of a hurricane, and she cried out with the pleasure of it as it consumed her. He thrust into her, as deeply as any lost cavern he'd ever penetrated, and she fell onto him again and again as he found his own release and shuddered into fulfillment.

She fell to one elbow, then slid off his body and into that warm spot beside him that in some wonderful way she was beginning to think of as hers.

"Cate," he sighed, and wrapped a lazy arm around her.

She found the presence of mind to locate the comforter and pull it up around their shoulders, and he snapped off the light.

"Feels like forever," she thought she heard him say.

The sound of his breathing told her he had slid into sleep almost before the words were out of his mouth.

It felt like forever, indeed.

For the next two days.

14

WHEN DANIEL WOKE, THE SUN hadn't yet lifted above the trees on the far side of the wetland, but already he could hear the racket as every bird in the place went about its business of getting breakfast and catching up on the gossip.

Cate still slept the sound sleep of the sexually satisfied—or so he could tell himself. Smiling, he got out of bed as quietly as he could, pulled on some clothes, and let himself out of their room to see if he could scare up some coffee. A bit of sweet talking with Dahlia Moreno, the owner's wife, convinced her to bring breakfast up on a tray to their room around eight.

She also poured him a cup of java from the huge pot on the counter in the kitchen.

"I suppose I have you to thank for the feminine touches like the rose on the pillow." He leaned on the counter and watched her take four trays of muffins—purple with fat berries—out of the double stack of ovens, one after the other.

Dahlia, who was built along the lines of his godmother and who seemed to have her knack with cooking, glanced at him as she turned the muffins out onto a cooling rack. "I wish I could take credit for it, but I can't. If you want roses on your pillow you need to go to the expensive places in San Francisco."

"No, I meant there was one. Yesterday afternoon, when we got back from a walk. A long-stemmed yellow rose." He sipped coffee. "I thought it was compliments of the house."

"Your book is around here somewhere," she said with a fine disregard for a writer's ego. "Maybe one of the staff read it and left a token of her appreciation."

"Maybe the same person who left her perfume on the bed?"

"I want to apologize again for that." With the muffins cooling in neat rows, she lined up a row of baskets on the counter and laid a fresh cloth in each one. "We're looking into it, you can be sure."

"You haven't seen anyone strange lurking around the place?"

"No more strange than the usual guests, tourists, hikers and lost people asking directions." One by one, the warm muffins went into the baskets. "A rose and some perfume. Sounds to me like you've got a fan."

"According to your husband, he or she is a jealous one. But unless they're a ghost who can walk through walls, I don't see how they could have got into the room. It was locked."

Dahlia shrugged. "No ghosts here, unfortunately. If we had one, we could be in the national registry and charge more. Muffin?"

"No thanks. How about a refill, and a second cup? Lots of cream."

"Help yourself. Bottomless cup. Rafael drinks it all day long. I'll have your tray up in half an hour or so."

Daniel collected the two mugs of coffee, thanked his hostess and climbed the stairs to their room. With typical California laissez-faire, nobody seemed to be making much of their perfume bandit. Nothing untoward had happened during the night, so the thing to do was forget it. After all, nothing had been damaged, and a guy certainly couldn't go to the cops complaining about a litterbug who dropped roses.

The smell of the hot coffee woke Cate. "Daniel? Is that coffee?"

"It is. Big and creamy, just the way you like it."

Her smile lit her face the way the sun was beginning to illuminate the world outside. "It's even better when it's in the hands of a sexy adventurer."

"With a taste for wicked women."

She laughed and sat up, then buried her nose in the mug. "Man, this is good."

"Compliments of Dahlia, who's making breakfast. She also says there's a copy of my book lying around here somewhere."

Cate grinned. "When you find it, you'll have to sign it. 'To Dahlia, whose coffee is to die for.'"

"Hopefully not. She says there are all kinds of strangers around here on a daily basis, so singling out our perfume bandit is a lost cause."

Cate shrugged, apparently more concerned about getting caffeine into her bloodstream than catching bandits.

"So, what do you feel like doing today?" He didn't

want to talk about stuff he couldn't answer. Everyone else's theories were going to have to do for now.

Cate sat back against the pillows, cradling her mug in both hands. "I want a great big breakfast and then a walk on the beach. Then I want to go to some touristy wharf and buy a silly souvenir for my admin, Anne, who is much too practical to do things like that for herself. After that I want to come back here and make love to you again, and then have supper." She smiled at him like a cat sunning itself on a soft cushion. "Doesn't that sound like a great day?"

"Except for the shopping on the wharf part, it does."

"Without the shopping part, the making love part doesn't happen," she warned him.

He held up his hands. "I give. You drive a hard bargain."

"It got me where I am today." She lay back more deeply, more seductively, in the pillows.

He put his mug down and stripped off his jeans.

She put her mug on the nightstand and lifted the comforter.

Neither of them heard Dahlia knock fifteen minutes later, or the sound of the tray being set down on the floor outside.

WHEN DANIEL GOT UP the second time, he practically tripped over the breakfast tray when he opened the door. Though the muffins were cold, they discovered, the omelets and hash browns were still warm—and the homemade salsa that came with them was so hot he broke into a sweat.

"Good stuff," he gasped, and sucked back a glass

of water from the bathroom to cool the heat from the chili peppers.

When they'd eaten and dressed, he made sure the windows were closed and the door was good and locked before they went downstairs. No more surprises for him, thanks—unless they were the kind that involved Cate in some state of undress.

The fog had pulled off the beach early and retreated to a fuzzy gray line on the horizon, leaving the sand washed by both intense summer light and the rolling surf. The waterline was marked by trails of kelp and bits of shell and polished glass, glinting in the sun. Daniel glanced behind them as Cate led the way down to the firm sand at the water's edge, and saw they had made a wavering line of footprints.

At some points there were two sets. At some points one. A perfect metaphor. Maybe even a sign that the time was right.

He reached out and took her hand as they walked slowly down the beach. "Cate."

"Look." She pointed at a flock of birds that looked like balls of fluff on Tinkertoy legs, running up and down the beach inches ahead of the waves. "Sandpipers."

Fascinating. "Cate, is there any chance you can get another week off?"

She dragged her gaze off the sandpipers and up to his face. "I only got these days because it's reading week, remember? I have to proctor exams next week."

A cozy vision of her going back with him and the two of them spending a week locked in his condo twisted like a plume of smoke and vanished on the wind. "Too bad. San Francisco is my last gig. I have some time off before my seniors come for the summer field trip so I was thinking we could hang out at my place in Long Beach." He pasted on a smile. "But never mind. It was just a thought."

Her penetrating gaze burned right through the fake smile and it melted off his lips. "What are you really saying, Daniel? We both know this isn't going to go any further. Why draw it out?"

Ouch. Talk about bone-scraping honesty. Well, at least he knew where he stood. "Are you so sure?"

She made a deprecating gesture with her free hand. "I know the kind of woman you like. Ones who are used to being in the spotlight and lead the same kind of exciting, adventurous life you do. Like that photographer. For a couple of days you and I can have fun together, but for the long term, I'm just not your kind of woman."

Just how shallow did she think he was? "Cate, you're a scientist, just like me. How much of what you think I am is a media creation and how much is based on your own observations?"

She pulled her hand from his and walked a little faster, but he had no trouble keeping up. "You don't seriously think I'd say something like that because I was going on something I'd read. Give me some credit. You said yourself you loved that photographer, and she jets off all over the world to take pictures in exciting and maybe dangerous locations. Maybe she's behind the camera instead of in front of it, but she's still part of the world you live in. And what do I do? I give lectures. I write papers. I have drinks with a friend once in a while. Big deal."

"I think it is a big deal. You've probably influenced more students in a positive way through your classes than I ever did picking leeches off my legs in the jungle."

"That's disgusting."

"That's reality. Leeches and lectures aside, I think we might have something together, Cate. I don't want it to be like last time, where we split up and go to the opposite ends of the country and never see each other again."

Her stride faltered, stopped. She stood and looked at him so long that the sandpipers stopped running ahead of them and began to probe the sand for whatever creatures they ate. Cate would probably know, but he didn't want to disturb what was going on behind those clear eyes by distracting her with a non sequitur. So he simply waited for her to speak.

"I'm afraid to think that you really mean it," she said at last.

That was an odd way to put it. "Anyone who climbs rocks doesn't know the meaning of fear."

"Anyone who climbs rocks takes appropriate steps for safety," she retorted. "Relationships are different. You don't get a rope or a net. Not even a good, strong knot to help you. You're on your own, stepping out into space to make a connection with another person."

"Ah, but that person is in the same place, stepping out to make a connection with you."

"Danger times two does not equal safety," she pointed out, but he felt a little optimistic when she took his hand and began walking back the way they'd come. She'd said she wanted to go shopping and then make love all afternoon when they got back. That was a good sign, wasn't it?

"But commitment to the stepping out might."

His unease lifted when she smiled up at him and squeezed his hand. "Touché. There goes my metaphor."

"I'm a practical guy. I'd rather plain talking than metaphor. And I'd rather have you in my life than any number of models, starlets or photographers. Even if it means I have to learn the names of every damn bird on the continent."

She swung their linked hands between them. "Is that why you have my picture in your briefcase?"

"How did you know that?" he said in surprise.

"I knocked it over the other day, and when I was putting all your stuff back, I saw the picture tucked into the lid."

And she'd never said a word until now. "Yes, I suppose it is. You were like my guiding light, in a way. Kept me from making some stupid decisions once or twice."

"How? When we hadn't seen each other in years and I left without giving you a thing?"

He shrugged, uncertain even in his own mind of his reasons. "I don't know. You were just so solid. So practical and so smart. I guess you were the standard I measured other women by. And, let's face it, I liked looking at your face."

He liked looking at it now, when the wind whipped her hair over her eyes and her cheeks were reddened with it—or maybe with what he'd been saying. He couldn't tell, and he wasn't about to ask.

"Well, if we're into true confessions, here, I guess

there's a reason I still have that copy of *Newsweek*," she admitted. "The photo was good enough to eat."

"How about the real thing?" he teased.

She laughed and picked up her pace, then began to run. "Definitely good enough to eat. Come on, I'll race you back to the hotel."

Maybe he'd get out of the shopping trip after all.

CATE SHRIEKED WITH LAUGHTER as Daniel grabbed her and tossed her on the bed. In the hour that they'd been down at the beach, housekeeping had come in and made it up, and there was no sign of either roses or perfume. Life was good. Cate landed in the middle of the comforter and rolled off it like a stuntwoman before Daniel landed on the bed himself.

He lay on his back and held out his arms. "Come on, babe. Just one kiss."

She backed away, shaking a finger. "Not a chance. I'm on to you. Don't think you can distract me with sex, mister. We're going shopping in Monterey and you're not getting out of it."

"Aw, man," he complained. Cate had the feeling that his feigned chagrin was actually real.

"Never mind. Adversity is good for you."

"But sex is better." He put his hands behind his head and stretched, just for her benefit, she had no doubt. Oh, yes, he made a very appealing picture, in those worn jeans. And his T-shirt did for his chest and abs what no T-shirt should do in civilized company.

But who said she was civilized? What she was was tempted.

Sex or shopping? Shopping or sex?

A month ago if anyone had told her she'd be in such a delicious dilemma, she'd have laughed at them. And now…well, it wasn't even a binary decision. There was no either/or. It was simply a matter of deciding which came first.

Delightful thought. "Don't worry, I'll stick to my promise," she told him. "Wharf first. I have to get something for Anne and I don't mean a T-shirt from the airport gift shop. After that you can bet I'm going to have my way with you, and there's no getting out of it."

"I love a strong-willed woman." He rolled to a sitting position on the edge of the bed. "But I'm not getting changed."

As if any woman passing by would complain about the sight he made. "Well, I am. Sweats are okay for the beach but I can't wear them into town. What if I met Clint Eastwood?"

"He'd be so dazzled by your smile and that thing your hips do when you walk, he wouldn't even notice your sweats."

She paused in the act of unzipping her suitcase. "That thing my hips do?"

"Mmm." His gaze took on the faraway look of a man reliving a wonderful memory.

"What thing?" Did she walk like a duck or something? Or worse—had the calories in the crème brûlée she'd devoured at supper last night relocated themselves to her butt so soon?

"That thing." He placed his hands a foot apart in the air and moved them back and forth in a hula rhythm. "I love that thing. Ever notice I walk behind you a lot?"

"Oh, you!" She snagged the pillow off the bed and fired it at him.

She stripped off her sweats and T-shirt and pulled a pair of stockings out of her bag. Sitting on the window seat with the glorious view of the wetland behind her and the planes of the old house's roof outside bouncing warmth onto her back, she pulled one stocking on.

"Oh, bother. I've got a run." She rummaged in a side pocket and found a second pair. The left toe had a hole in it, and a run was beginning there, too. Okay, on to plan B. Ditch the skirt and go with her black slacks. She had a fun little Azria flowered top that would go with them.

She pulled the slacks on and walked past Daniel. "There is no hip thing happening here," she told him. "See?"

"Oh, yes, there is." He gave her a thorough and appreciative once-over. "You can't help—oh-oh."

That didn't sound good. "What, oh-oh?" She twisted around, trying to see over her shoulder. "Are they dirty?"

"No, but it looks as though the pressure is too much for 'em. You have a split down the back."

"What? These are brand new!"

She had them off in two seconds, convinced he was teasing her, but he was right. The stitches had parted down the back of her slacks, and would have given all of Monterey a lovely view of her royal-blue undies if it hadn't been for Daniel and his "hip thing."

"Good grief. I wonder when that happened? I had them on at the conference and I'm positive they were all right."

She hoped.

No, someone would have said something. Never mind. On to plan C.

"Clint will just have to make do with my trusty jeans," she said. "I have some skirts and blouses but the shoes that go with them are meant for business lunches and cocktail parties, not tramping around on wharves and beaches."

Luckily she'd only worn her tailored white shirt once, and had folded it carefully. She shook it out and shrugged it on, then went to do up the buttons.

Her fingers slid down an empty placket.

She held both sides of the shirt taut and stared at it. "Daniel, all my buttons are gone."

"What?" He got up and came over to look.

"Look. All the buttons have been snipped off this shirt. See, some of the threads are still here."

She looked around a little blankly, half expecting to see the buttons come rolling across the floor.

"Wait a minute." Daniel held up a hand and ticked off items. "Holes in both pairs of stockings. A hole in your slacks. Buttons cut off your shirt." He reached into her suitcase and lifted out the small but efficient pile of her clothes. "Cate, you'd better check everything."

A cold, sick feeling made of outrage and hurt settled into her stomach as one by one she cataloged the damage.

The stitches on one sleeve of her flowered Azria top had been picked out, leaving it hanging from the arm hole.

The hem of her black skirt drooped.

And what looked like a blackberry from one of their muffins had been mashed into the front of her white wraparound blouse, rendering it unwearable now and, without bleach, for the foreseeable future.

"Daniel, all my clothes," she said in a tone halfway between a whisper and a wail. "Everything but what I had on. Everything's ruined."

He was holding her flowered top as though it were the body of a loved one. "Not ruined."

She stared at him. "What do you mean, not? There isn't one thing in this suitcase I can wear!"

"Remember what you said to me yesterday? That it must be a woman doing this because the damage can be easily fixed?" He indicated the blouse he held. "Look at this. A few seconds with a sewing machine and it's as good as new. Same with your skirt and slacks. The stain can be bleached out, and stockings are cheap. This person could have taken a pair of shears and shredded everything in the room, but she didn't. She just made it temporarily impossible for you to wear your clothes."

"Great. Kind of like the difference between harassment and murder. Neither of which is acceptable."

Her voice shook with anger and the inescapable sense that someone had set out to hurt her though she'd done them no harm. Someone had invaded her privacy, hunted through her things, and then taken the time to snip threads and poke holes, carefully damaging everything just enough that in some cases, such as the slacks and the skirt hem, perhaps it wouldn't even be noticed until it was too late and Cate was out in public.

"I've had enough of this." Daniel put the blouse on the bed and called the manager, Rafael Moreno. When he arrived not sixty seconds later, Daniel showed him Cate's clothes.

"I want to talk to your housekeeping staff immediately," Daniel told him in the kind of voice that made archaeology students hop to their duties with no whining or argument. "And once I've done that, we're leaving and filing a complaint with the sheriff's office."

Moreno looked as though he were about to weep. "The Egret Inn will of course reimburse Ms. Wells for all the damage her things have sustained," he said. "In fact, my mother is a seamstress. If you would like to take the time, I can have your clothes repaired immediately."

"That's not—"

"Thank you, Mr. Moreno, that's very kind." Cate interrupted. "If she can do it while you and Daniel are interviewing the staff, then at least I'll have a few things and won't have to go out and spend the money to replace them."

It wasn't likely that she'd find another Azria blouse here in the bird sanctuary, and it was one of her favorites, bought last year during the fall sale at Saks. If the elder Mrs. Moreno could put the sleeve back in, Cate wasn't going to argue.

Daniel visibly bit back what he had been going to say and watched her gather up everything that could be repaired.

"If you like, I can also have the white blouse laundered," Moreno offered. "Everything will be returned to you by two o'clock, you have my word."

"Thank you, that's very kind." Cate added her blouse to the pile.

"And now I'd like to talk to your staff," Daniel said grimly.

"Yes, of course. There is myself, my wife, and our daughter Galina and her cousin Ana, who maintain the rooms. Our son Jose is groundskeeper."

A family business. Built from the ground up with hard work, elbow grease, great cooking and word of mouth. Cate began to see what damage a complaint to the local sheriff would incur here. The damage to her own belongings was insignificant in comparison—and as Daniel had said, there was nothing so bad there that the Moreno family could not repair it and make it as good as new.

"Daniel, I don't think it's necessary to—" She stopped and bent down near the window seat. "Look, here's one of my shirt buttons." The buttons were mother-of-pearl chips and had caught the light when she'd moved. She'd thought they'd be at the bottom of her suitcase, but evidently their burglar had carried them around while she was inflicting her damage.

Another wink of light came from the windowsill. "Look, here's another one."

"What are they doing there?" Daniel took the little circle of shell and examined it.

Cate looked out of their window, which was a dormer set in the roof. The light caught another button, lying on the shingle. "There's one out there, too."

"What did she do, cut them off your shirt and then throw them out the window?"

Cate pulled up the sash and leaned out. She looked from the button on the shingle to the roof, then craned around to look up the slope behind the dormer.

And then she saw what was happening.

"Daniel, it isn't the maids that have been doing this. I bet it's another guest. And she didn't come through a locked door, either." She pulled her head back in and straightened. "She's been coming over the roof." She looked Mr. Moreno in the eye. "I bet we'll find our culprit in the other room with a dormer window."

15

INDIANA JONES OR NOT, Daniel had never met a roof he didn't like.

While Cate and the manager went to find out who was booked into the room with the matching window on the other side of the house, he simply dropped onto the warm gray shingles from theirs and went soft-footed up the east slope to the peak of the roof and over the other side.

Yep, it could be done, and in less than thirty seconds. This was the kind of escape route that all the bad guys took in old movies and that had fallen out of use now that windows in hotels and office buildings were no longer designed to open.

Their target's room was empty, and while he waited, he surveyed the world from this unusual vantage point. Cars went past on the highway half a mile away, creating a susurration similar to the wash of the waves on the beach. Directly below, a young man came out the back door with a bundle of clothes in a tote bag, a familiar flowered blouse on top. He got into an ancient Datsun and accelerated down the driveway like a man on a mission.

A sound in the room behind him made Daniel turn. Through the glass, he watched Moreno let Cate in, and she slid up the sash for him. He swung himself into a room very similar to their own, with the bed neatly made up and fresh towels folded in fluffy white bundles in the bathroom.

"She checked out this morning, didn't she?" he said.

Moreno nodded. "The party was registered as Admiral and Mrs. Baldwin, but only Mrs. Baldwin checked in two nights ago. She said her husband had been detained at Moffett Field and she was to meet him in San Diego."

"An admiral's wife?" Cate had been prowling the edges of the room, no doubt looking for the rest of her buttons, but the carpets had been vacuumed and everything already wiped down by either Galina or Ana. "That doesn't sound like the kind of person who'd be climbing over roofs and cutting up people's clothes."

"I doubt she was an admiral's wife and she probably wasn't going to San Diego," Daniel said. "It looks as though you were right, Cate. A crazed fan. An anonymous loony. But she's gone now, so she probably got her ya-yas out on your stuff and that's the end of it."

"Does this mean you will be staying with us tonight as planned?" Mr. Moreno said, hope in his eyes.

Daniel glanced at Cate and saw the answer. "I'm afraid not, Mr. Moreno."

How could any woman feel safe in the inn after an invasion like this? Granted, it wasn't as if they'd been mugged and left for dead. But the precise malice and deliberate damage, aimed specifically at Cate, creeped even him out, and with everything he'd seen, that was hard to do.

Moreno's face fell with disappointment, and Cate stepped forward and laid a gentle hand on his arm. "But we certainly won't be going to the police. The woman didn't fill out the space for a license plate on the registration form, and if the name is a fake, there's nothing we could tell them anyway."

"But we have lost your trust," Moreno said. And clearly cared about it. Daniel had to admire the guy.

"Not our trust. We're a little shaken up, but you've gone above and beyond to make things right," he said. "I was angry earlier, and I apologize. There's nothing we can learn here, but while we wait for Cate's clothes to come back I'd like to talk to your daughter or your niece, whichever one dossed down this room."

Moreno nodded and went out, and in a moment they heard him call downstairs in Spanish. A young woman of about twenty, wearing her thick, glossy hair in a French braid, joined them a couple of minutes later.

"I'm Galina," she said, shaking hands with him and Cate. "Everyone's talking about what happened. I'm so sorry."

"I am, too. Can you tell us if you noticed anything unusual when you cleaned this room this morning?"

Galina's brown eyes were thoughtful as she gazed around the room, as if visualizing it the way it had been earlier. "The lady was out all day, and when she was here, she took her meals in her room. I didn't notice anything different about her—lots of people come here to get away, even from other people in the dining room."

"What did she look like?" Cate asked.

Galina shrugged. "Tall, blond. A *Norteamericano* complexion—you know, doesn't take the sun well. Her nose was peeling and so were her earlobes. A good advertisement for sunblock, if you ask me."

"It also could describe a thousand women here on vacation from cooler places," Daniel pointed out.

"Perhaps a clue could be found in what she left behind in the trash," Mr. Moreno suggested. "Did you look?"

"No, I didn't even think of it." Galina crossed to the door. "I've only done her room so far, so the skip won't have much in it. Back in a sec."

There wasn't much any of them could do while they waited. Daniel took Cate's hand and gave it a reassuring squeeze. Her fingers were cold and her mouth was tense.

They were definitely pulling out of here and checking in to someplace that had security cameras and key cards. No more old-fashioned, romantic ambience for him, thank you very much.

Galina was back in five minutes carrying a small white garbage bag. She turned its contents out onto the mirrored tray in the bathroom that had held a selection of shampoo and soaps. Daniel looked over Cate's shoulder. Two tissues, an empty lipstick, a few hairs of a color that could be anything from brown to auburn... and a bottle of wash-in hair coloring in a shade called Platinum Ash.

"Great," Cate said. "She wasn't even a blonde. So the only true thing we know about her is that her nose and earlobes are sunburned." Cate glanced at Daniel. "I guess it's a good thing we didn't embarrass ourselves down at the sheriff's department. Hey, what's that?" Several small objects had clattered from Galina's hand onto the tray. "There's the rest of my buttons."

"At least she's not totally psycho." At Cate's inquiring look, Daniel went on, "You know, keeping these for a trophy."

"Is this woman dangerous?" Galina wanted to know.

Daniel shook his head. "I doubt it. On the nutso continuum, she's pretty mild. Considerate. Tidy, even, taking the buttons with her instead of throwing them around the room."

"If we had to have a stalker, it's nice that she's considerate." Cate's tone was slightly less chilly than, say, the wind off the polar ice cap. "Thank you, Mr. Moreno, Galina, for helping us with this. Do you think you might call over to your mother and see where she is with the repairs?"

"If you give me the buttons, I will take them to her and inquire personally."

While Mr. Moreno hustled off and Galina tidied up the unknown woman's room a second time, Daniel took Cate across the landing and down the hall to their own room. Once the door was firmly closed, Cate turned and he saw that the tension inside her was about to snap.

"Is this normal for you?" she asked, her lips tight and her arms crossed over her chest. "Does this kind of thing happen so often that you can make jokes about it?"

Jokes? "Cate, your estimation of this person yesterday was correct and I was just emphasizing that. She's not only considerate in her attention-getting destructive behavior, she's tidy."

"You should be the one on *CSI*. The only people giving me any real help here are Galina and Mr. Moreno's mother."

He squelched the hurt before it could ignite his temper and spoke in a tone of reasonable calm. "It's my nature to make up theories. I know they don't help, but they give me the illusion that I have some control."

The tightly crossed arms loosened and she pushed her hair behind her ears with both hands. "I'm sorry. You're right." She sat on the neatly made bed and stared glumly at her empty suitcase. "I hate not having control."

It was probably safe to sit beside her. He put an arm around her shoulders. "Your things will be as good as new—or better, if Mr. Moreno has anything to say about it. The nutcase is gone and not likely to come back. We'll get out of here and head up to Oakland and find a big, anonymous hotel where even we won't be able to find our room. How does that sound?"

A smile flickered on her mouth and he breathed again. He hated the feeling of not being in control himself, and what he hated even more was the fact that he hadn't been able to protect Cate—or even her clothes—from the fictitious Mrs. Baldwin. He hadn't even known there was a threat, and when Cate had offered a theory, he'd shot it down without giving it a thought.

So much for the modern, liberated man.

"You haven't answered me." Cate took a deep breath and straightened, and Daniel yanked himself out of his depressing thoughts.

"Sorry. What was your question?"

"Whether this was normal for you."

He huffed a soundless laugh. "Hardly. Oh, I get notes and little gifts at the odd book signing, and my assistant has to deal with some non-business e-mail at school, but that's about the extent of it. I've never had a stalker before." An idea occurred to him. "Or maybe it's not even my stalker. Maybe she was yours. Ticked anybody off lately?"

She drew her chin in and stared at him. "Me? Nobody knows I exist, and thank God for that. You're the one charming everyone's socks off on national television."

"And for this I get a stalker."

"Clearly she's yours and not mine. She didn't harm you in any way. In fact, the rose was probably some kind of conciliatory gesture—an apology to you before she went to work to scare me off."

"Which didn't happen."

Cate was silent, and the breeze coming in through the still-open window blew cold on his skin.

"CATE?"

Her emotions were such a mixed-up brew of anger, fear, desire and need that all Cate wanted to do was to throw herself into Daniel's arms and cry.

She was sick and tired of always having to be the strong one, of always being the leader—of classes, of symposia, even of her damn book group. Sure, she liked to be in control, but didn't everyone like to have that sense that their hand was on the steering wheel of their own life? Cate was just plain tired of driving alone. She wanted to climb into Daniel's 1968 Camaro and have nothing more to think about than what the wind was doing to her hair.

Except that she was afraid to. It was one thing to

decide on a fling with a celebrity that was guaranteed to end inside of a week. It was quite another thing to become involved with a real man—one who wanted a real relationship.

Because look what happened when she allowed *that*. Disaster. Or desertion. Or both.

She made a little sound halfway between a hiccup and a sob.

"Cate?" Hiccup. Sniffle. "Honey, what is it?" Deep breath. Wail. "Aw, come here." Daniel gathered her into his arms and she caved into his hard chest and let the dam break.

The ugly truth was that she was "—just a coward—" she said incoherently into his T-shirt, and the whole damn conversation about "—groupies or stalkers or whatever—" was just an excuse because she was afraid, "—afraid, Daniel—" to get into relationships because the guy always said she wasn't good enough and they "—always leave and I just know—" he'd leave, too, and if she gave her heart again she just "—couldn't stand it!"

"Shhh," he soothed, stroking her back while she cried and let the horrible, immature, embarrassing truth spill out of her.

God, it felt good to get it all out there at last. What she needed was a shot of courage, and maybe she could find it right here in his arms. After all, he hadn't asked for her whole life, had he? He'd just asked for a chance. And if people like the mysterious Mrs. Baldwin were the exception rather than the rule, then maybe she could get past the whole dating-a-celebrity thing and the he's-going-to-dump-me thing and actually have something real.

Look on the bright side. Maybe the next book will tank and he'll go back to being a normal, everyday archaeologist.

She took a long, shaky breath and straightened her spine. He loosened his hold enough to slide his hands down her arms, and gripped her fingers. She'd always loved his hands. After these few days together, she could count the reasons why.

"Okay?" he asked, his sober gaze on hers.

She nodded.

"You're not going to dump me on my head and take a bus to the airport?"

"No. But I sure wish we'd hear from Mr. Moreno's mother."

As if in answer, they heard the sound of a couple of vehicles pulling into the driveway below, and in a moment, Mr. Moreno knocked on the door of their room. When Cate opened it, he presented her with the neat stack of clothes.

"The berry stain on the white blouse will take a little more time," he said apologetically. "Perhaps as late as this afternoon."

"That's okay." She dug a card out of her bag and gave it to him. "Just send it to that address. I can live without it for the rest of the week."

Amid a flurry of packing, apologies, credit-card receipts and a box lunch for the road courtesy of Dahlia Moreno, they got under way at last. Cate had never been so grateful for the push of the wind in her face and the vibration of an engine under her feet as Daniel gunned the Camaro up the ramp and onto the highway.

"Next time," she said to Daniel, "I get to pick the hotel."

He glanced at her and raised an eyebrow. "Does that mean there's going to be a next time? Other than the anonymous chain hotel with key cards for tonight, that is?"

She laid her hand on his knee and he covered it with his free one. "I think so. I don't think I'm going to run away this time, Daniel."

He squeezed her hand so hard her fingers were crushed together. Then he seemed to realize what he was doing and loosened his grip. "I'm glad. Even with the stalkers and fans and *Jah-Redd?*"

"I won't lie to you—I'm not comfortable with any of them. But I am interested in you and what you are deep inside. The external stuff will come and go, but if you're serious about something happening between us, that's less important than the connection we make. Just between us two."

"What about you?" he asked. "Any rabid ex-boyfriends or psycho department heads to tell me about?"

She laughed and pushed her hair out of her eyes. "As a matter of fact…" It only took about ten miles to tell the sad story of Charles and his past and future wife, and then give brief sketches of Byron and Robert. "My love life hasn't been nearly as interesting as yours," she confessed finally. "Though considering recent events, maybe that's not a bad thing."

"Believe me, recent events don't have anything to do with my love life."

"What makes you say that?"

"For one thing, no one I ever dated knew a button from a seam, much less how to detach a sleeve."

"I don't think you need to know how to sew to snip threads."

"And I'm not in the habit of leaving messages with roses, so it's not like that was intended to say anything specifically about a relationship."

Cate disagreed, but she let it pass.

"Besides, who knew I was here? Nobody except Stacy Mills, and she wasn't at the hotel."

"Do we know that for sure?"

He glanced at her. "Cate, give the poor girl a break. She's been working her butt off on this book tour. She doesn't have time to check in to romantic hideaways to climb over roofs and snip clothes apart."

She had to admit that was probably true.

"We should talk about the future," she said as they passed long fields full of mature artichokes and rows of young green strawberries. "If not now, then sometime."

"You're going to pin me down when the only thing I know for sure about my life is that it's scheduled through Thursday?"

"That is such a guy thing to say. What's wrong with wanting to look at the future?"

Planning comforted her. She was the kind who began packing her suitcase two weeks before she left on a trip. This was why she always arrived with everything she needed and never forgot anything. She always researched a destination, finding out where the hotels were, what kind of transportation there was and all the things there were to do. And once she knew that, she planned out her days and made reservations well in advance.

Julia Covington called her a control freak. Talk about

the pot calling the kettle black. She was simply a practical person who liked to be prepared.

"Nothing at all. There was a time when those words coming out of a woman's mouth would have made me stop at the nearest gas station and then take off when she was in the restroom."

"And now?" Cate knew the answer but she still wanted to hear it again. As if every time he said it, it became a little more real.

"I was the one who brought it up. I meant it then and I mean it now. It's almost the end of the school year. Once you get your exam results in and your paperwork wrapped up, maybe you'd give some thought to coming to Turkey with me. They're doing some really interesting work at a site there, and you might get some data about your feminine cults."

Turkey? He was going all the way to Turkey? Goodness, she was going to have to start researching the archaeological work currently going on over there as soon as she got home.

"How long will you be there?" she asked.

"Just a month. We could cut it to three weeks if you were there, though, and do a bit of tripping if you wanted. It'll be too hot to stay in the Aegean, but we could go up into the mountains in Greece. Delphi is spectacular in the summer."

"I've never been to Delphi. Maybe I'll find an oracle and she'll do a better job at telling me about your future than you do."

He made a self-deprecating face. "I thought I was doing well to know what the next couple of months hold."

She patted his knee. "You are. But I'm the kind of person who likes to plan. Maybe it's that need to be in the driver's seat—you know, thinking I have control of my time, at least."

"Just don't forget to plan for a little spontaneity."

She had to laugh. With Daniel, that wasn't going to be a problem.

16

AT THE HUGE HOTEL IN OAKLAND, Daniel carried their bags down the long hallway and waited while Cate opened the door of their room. All the way up the coast from the Egret Inn, he'd kept one eye on the traffic behind them, in case he could single out any one vehicle that seemed to be following. But there'd been nothing. No familiar faces at the gas station in San Jose and none in the hotel lobby.

As far as he could figure, there was nothing preventing them from making love immediately and ordering room service afterward.

Cate opened the curtains and took in the view of the bay, with the Golden Gate Bridge stitching two points of land together in the distance. "Look at that." She pointed to the side. "There's an outdoor art fair in the parking lot next door. Since we skipped Monterey, maybe I can get something for Anne there."

Nothing except a woman's need to shop, which overrode all other biological imperatives.

At least she was efficient. After fifteen minutes of browsing in the white canvas stalls and chatting with the artists, Cate had narrowed her list down to a necklace made from glass beads that looked like spun-sugar candy and a watercolor of the Golden Gate.

"Decisions, decisions," she mused. "If I get her the necklace, then at least I can enjoy it, too, when she wears it to work."

Daniel knew when his opinion wasn't necessary, so he kept his mouth shut and his mind on the picture of Cate doing something frivolous and—to her—fun. This wasn't Dr. Wells, the driven academic. Or Cate the athletic rock climber and bird chaser. This was just Cate in her simplest form, buying a gift for a friend.

Maybe, if these growing emotions inside him had their way, this would be the Cate he'd see most often on a daily basis. The loving person made happy when she was able to delight someone else.

The way she delighted him when they were skin to skin, or he was buried so deeply in her body he could no longer imagine what it would be like with another woman. She was no longer the angry academic with the fanged bunny slippers. She was a woman who knew what she wanted—and even better, wanted it with him.

"I'm starving," Cate announced when they got back to their room.

"I have an idea." He found the room-service card. "Let's get naked and eat dinner in bed." He'd never eaten a steak dinner in bed in his life, but if a person was going to do it, then a chain hotel was the place.

And Cate didn't even hesitate. By the time room service got there with the trolley, she'd stripped and jumped under the sheets. Fortunately the kitchen whipped up a fine steak, and sharing every other bite with Cate while sneaking choice bits of salad away from her was kind of fun.

"If we get steak juice on these sheets, you're sleeping on the wet spot." Cate pointed a julienned strip of red pepper at him and then ate it.

"If we do that, we're calling housekeeping. And you get to explain what the stain is."

He couldn't remember the last time he'd goofed around with someone like a couple of kids with their parents out of town for the weekend. He wasn't a serious kind of guy. Why, then, had his relationships lacked laughter and this companionable sparkle? With Dulcie Cavanaugh in particular the sex had been driven, reverent, almost, though she was a cheery person in other facets of her life. He'd cared about her, cared a lot, and it hadn't bothered him until now, when he could contrast her dark linen sheets and shuttered windows with this bright room and the cutlery and napkins scattered within reach.

With Cate, he could be himself. She knew his mistakes and his memories. She knew the public guy and the private one. And maybe that was part of it. The boy who read comic books about a superhero's adventures had become the man who traveled the world in his own. But deep inside there was still that boy who loved to laugh and make jokes, and dream about what lay over that horizon.

Cate didn't laugh at that boy, because inside her was a girl who did the same thing, who loved birds for their ability to fly away and see what was out there, yet had her feet firmly planted on the ground.

"We should go to Turkey together." He leaned back against the pillows and watched her polish off some dessert that involved a lot of raspberry sauce.

"And this is apropos of what?" she said around her spoon.

"Apropos of the two of us always wanting to know what's over the horizon. We both have this thing about being tied to the earth—even though we spend our lives digging in it."

Cate put the spoon down and began to collect all their dishes and stack them on the tray. "Is this a gentle way of leading up to the 'I don't want to be tied down' speech?"

He stared at her. "Not at all. I was just thinking about you and your cliffs and birds and me always wanting to be in the field. Which led me to thinking about Turkey. No puns or implications meant."

"You don't want to be in the field all the time, though, do you?" She carried the tray out and deposited it in the hallway, then climbed back under the sheets with him. "Because while I like an annual expedition as much as the next person, I'm kind of a homebody. Papers have to be written sometime."

"I know they do. Well, let's compromise, then. Two expeditions a year. And maybe one less paper."

"Deal." She snuggled down next to him, and he slid lower on the pillows so he could put an arm around her. "It seems funny to be talking like this when a week ago I'd just seen your name in the conference flyer. And that woman, Morgan Shaw, came into my office with that carved box."

"A lot of things can change in a week." A spurt of

adrenaline shot through his gut, as though he were a diver on a cliff, looking down into the deep blue water. Then he leaped. "A guy could fall in love, for instance."

She went absolutely still against his side. "Could he?"

What did this mean? Didn't she feel the same? Had he taken the leap, only to discover the tide had gone out and there was really nothing to land on but rocks?

"Maybe," he said, preparing to backpedal.

"There's one more thing we need to add to the deal."

To avoid the rocks, he was pretty much ready to agree to anything. "What's that?"

"This whole celebrity angle."

"I know it bugs you."

She propped herself up on one elbow. "It's not that it bugs me. It throws the wrong kind of light on the discipline, Daniel. As in, a massive klieg light."

"We can use some light. And you know that public acceptance of my work brings in more funding."

"But Daniel, you don't have to do these appearances with starlets to get public acceptance or funding. You don't have to make yourself look like a glory-hound to get respect."

Her breathing was fast and those telltale streaks of color had appeared on her cheekbones. Fight or flight. Well, after the big meal they'd just consumed, he didn't want to do either one. Instead, he pulled her down beside him, where she lay stiffly, unwilling to soften.

"Cate, tell me what's really behind this. I agree I can probably lose the starlets. I'd rather have you at my side. But there's something else that's eating you. How about you tell me what it is?"

She was silent for a moment, and then with a sigh her body began to relax.

"Fear, I guess. You wouldn't believe how stuffy they are at Vandenberg. I guess I'm afraid that if our names are linked in the press, the dean will trot out his morality lecture and I won't get what I've been working toward all these years."

"What's that? Tenure?"

"Yes."

"Do you really want tenure under conditions like that? Where you can't maintain a personal life?"

"There's a difference between having a personal life and having one splashed all over the tabloids. And believe me, lots of the faculty read them, though they'd die before they said so."

"I can't believe it." He gave her a little squeeze. "A bunch of scientists? What happened to reliable data and reputable sources?"

"I know." Her voice was muffled between the pillow and his shoulder. "You should have heard me bad-mouthing you over the *Newsweek* article, and that's not even sold on the same shelf. Now I'm going to have to take it all back and admit that—"

"What?"

"—that I've fallen for you after all."

17

CATE HAD LEARNED THE HARD WAY that, sometimes, the consequences of saying the words were harder to live with than actually having the relationship. With Charles, the words had been the catalyst that had triggered his flight to Chicago and back to his wife. In one way that was a good thing. Maybe she'd done him a favor. In another way, it was totally humiliating to realize that he'd rather have a woman he'd left once already than have her.

Most of the time, Cate preferred to think it was the first option.

As for Byron and Robert, she'd taken them seriously at the time, but she could see now they were more like practice climbs—the walls you scaled when you were getting ready for the real thing. She hadn't gotten very far, but at least she'd honed her skills before Daniel had come along.

And in a funny way, she supposed she could be grateful for that, too.

Their conversation the night before had cleared the air between her and Daniel, and the California weather seemed to reflect it. After breakfast in the restaurant off the hotel's lobby, they took the shuttle downtown to

Jack London Square. The place was alive with groups of people strolling in the sun, sleek sailboats scudding by on the bay, and gulls wheeling and calling to each other as the ferries plied the waters beneath them.

She felt the way a cat must feel after a full meal, lying in the sun and blinking with contentment. Even her skin felt smoother, her muscles silkier, as though sex had performed some kind of magic on her. Or maybe it was more than sex. More than learning the heights to which pleasure could take her. Maybe it was simply being in love.

Could that be possible? Could she really have fallen in love with Daniel in such a short time? Because she'd never believed in love at first sight. In her rational way, she'd always believed that friendship deepened into love, the way it had with her parents. Infatuation, yes. Lust, of course. Those were the work of a couple of seconds. But real love?

Oh, Cate, tell yourself the truth. You've been in love with Daniel Burke for eight years and this is the first chance you've had to express it...or even really to experience it.

On an unfamiliar cliff, her natural tendency was to examine a handhold from all sides, tap it and make sure it was solid before she trusted herself to it. But could she do that with love? She'd been perfectly willing to throw herself into a fling without a safety net. What about when the future wasn't so cut and dried? When it couldn't be planned out and analyzed in advance? What then?

When not one, not two, but three men did a double take and turned to look at her as she walked past them on her way to the newspaper kiosk in the center of the square. Despite her pensive thoughts, she grinned to herself. As Daniel would say, that was repeatable data.

She had definitely changed, both inside and out. And from the looks of it, her outside was looking the way her insides felt—happy and sated and beautiful. Maybe she should just go with it for once and see where it took her. Maybe take a leaf from Daniel's book and stop organizing everything to death.

Maybe one of the wonderful things about love was that you couldn't plan it. You could only enjoy it.

When Daniel stopped to speak to a guy in a three-piece suit who was feeding the pigeons, she glanced at the papers and ragmags festooned all over the kiosk. Dr. Hoogbeck's fossils might have garnered a headline or two. If so, she'd keep the article. She wasn't about to turn into a scrapbooker or anything, but it would be a souvenir of the conference where her life had been changed as irrevocably as had that cliff below the conference center.

Thieves Lift Star Amulet from New York Auction House.

Bay Area Wetlands Endangered by Airport Development.

Real Indiana Jones: Secret Love Nest.

Flash Mob Turns into Riot: Aliens Responsible?

Wait a minute. What was that? Cate snatched the glossy tabloid out of its metal rack and feverishly turned to the article inside—which turned out to be the centerfold.

Pop archaeologist Daniel Burke (photo, left) has long been known for his dazzling discoveries and

appeal for the ladies. But has the real-life adventurer finally decided to forego the Hollywood
lovelies and settle down with a homegrown
honey? And just who is the mysterious, leggy
beauty whom Burke spirited off to a well-known
honeymoon hideaway?

See our exclusive photo story on these pages
and judge for yourself: Is this the woman who will
finally capture the real Indiana Jones?

Cate's entire body seemed to be freezing over with
cold horror, one piece at a time. The sunny, noisy
square faded into silence as she gaped at the pictures
in the spread.

The Camaro, parked on the side of the highway
with only Daniel's knees visible as he knelt on the
ground. All the reader could see of Cate was one leg
flung over the back of the seat and a hand gripping it.
From this angle, it was easy to speculate what was
going on, though.

The next photo showed the two of them in a long-
distance shot in the bird sanctuary, wrapped around
each other in a kiss. This time it was Daniel who was
obscured, but Cate's entire back view filled the frame,
including her foot wrapped around his knee.

Lovely. Could the fact that she couldn't wait to get
back to the hotel to jump him be any more graphic?

Apparently, it could. The final shot had to have been
taken by someone standing on the roof of the bed-and-
breakfast hotel, right outside their window. It showed
her and Daniel, naked—though pertinent body parts

had been blurred out by the newspaper's editors—and she was craning up while—oh, God—Daniel very suggestively fed her a banana. Her face was clearly visible.

Instantly recognizable.

Was that why those three men had turned to look at her? One of them had spun so fast he'd lost his hat—and he'd been carrying a paper. Had it been this one? Did everyone in Jack London Square know she was Daniel's "homegrown honey"? Were they all speculating about the way she'd deep-throated that banana?

Scalding blood cascaded into her cheeks, her neck, her chest—it felt as if her whole body were blushing, or had been dipped into the hot acid of humiliation. How could this have happened? Who could possibly have done such a thing to them? Just how much malice was it possible to contain and still masquerade as a human being?

Because of course it had to have been their rose-dropping, perfume-wielding burglar.

Cate clutched the paper closer and scanned the type for a byline. It had been written by some scum-peddling hack named Jason Castro, but where was the photo credit? Where, where, wh—

Photos by D. N. Cavanaugh.

The rush of shame faded, to be replaced by the cool clarity of confirmation. "The ones I really like don't get into the papers," Daniel said in her memory, probably within hours of that fatal banana photograph. Cate lowered the paper slowly.

What had she ever done to Dulcie Cavanaugh? If she had something against Daniel, why was she attacking Cate?

"Lady, you mess that paper up any more you're going to have to buy it." The news agent leaned out of his kiosk window and gave her the hairy eyeball.

She pulled a dollar out of her bag and handed it to him, then turned without another word and headed blindly across the square. Some vague instinct directed her to go back to her hotel room, to pull the covers over her head and hide until it was time to go home and—

Oh, my God.

Home. The university. The newsstand on the corner where half the faculty furtively bought the paper on their way into class in the morning. The students. The department chair.

Cate imagined the laughter and the derision once it got out, as it surely would. Nobody admitted to reading the tabloids but everyone seemed completely on top of what was in them.

She looked with horror at the paper in her hands. Her career at Vandenberg was over.

Her cell phone rang and she jumped as though she'd been caught in the act of doing something illegal. She dug it out of her bag and answered it in a tone halfway between a whisper and a squeak.

"Cate?" Anne Walters said. "Cate, is that you?"

"Yes."

"Are you in a library or something? Do you want to call me back?"

Cate spared a moment of fond regret for a life when her biggest excitement was going to the opening of the New York Library's latest exhibition.

"No, it's okay. I'm in Oakland. Outside. What's up?"

"I thought you'd like to know about your messages."

Why? Her life had just imploded. Who cared what was on Anne's neatly written yellow slips? "I'll be back in the office Thursday. I don't think—"

"No, Cate. You don't get it. You really need to hear about these."

Something in Anne's tone sent up a warning flag. "All right. I'm listening."

"First of all, there's a reminder of the staff meeting Thursday afternoon at three. Morgan Shaw has called twice since you've been gone—please call her ASAP about the photographs of the box."

The photos. The ones that had precipitated her visit out here. She'd forgotten all about them.

"Your mom and dad are going to be in town at the end of the month and your mom wants to know if you can get tickets to *Spamalot.*"

"Is she kidding?" Cate asked blankly.

"I know. I told her. Dennis Dileone wants to know if you can proctor his Greek history exam next week, and Darlene Goldberg in the bookstore says the textbooks you wanted for the fall semester have gone out of print and what's plan B."

"Anne, tell me again why these couldn't have waited until I got home?" *I need to go find a cave to hide in for the rest of my life and you're holding me up.*

"That was just the warm-up." Anne took a deep breath. "Have you seen *Entertainment News* this week?"

Cate looked down at the paper in her hands. "I have it right here."

"Look on page twenty-four."

"I already did. What's the damage?" When Anne was silent, Cate swallowed. "Come on, Anne. You need to tell me before I walk in there on Thursday and get eaten alive."

Anne made a squeaking noise.

"Anne? Are you there?"

"I'm here. Bad choice of words, considering this picture. How old is that car?"

Cate's knees gave out. "It's not what you think." *Liar*.

"I might believe you, but Dr. Trowbridge doesn't. He's calling you up for a disciplinary review, Cate. Says you're—" her voice dropped an octave "—bringing this institution into disrepute." Her voice returned to normal. "I called Saks to see if they had anything in Kevlar, but they don't."

"Disciplinary review?"

She was going to be fired. No one had been called in for a review in all the time she'd been at Vandenberg. Personnel problems were solved within the department, at most with a transfer or reassignment to one of the satellite colleges. But when the department head took it to the dean of humanities, it meant trouble.

The kind of trouble that canceled all hope of tenure and ended careers.

"Is there anything I can do?" Anne's sense of humor had deserted her and she sounded close to tears.

Cate shook her head, then remembered Anne couldn't see her. "Just scoop up any copies of that paper that are lying around and put them through the shredder."

"How did it happen?"

"Hell hath no fury. How else?"

Anne drew a breath. "An old girlfriend out for revenge?"

"Who happens to be a professional photographer. I have a feeling she won't be putting this job on her résumé, though."

As she said goodbye and turned off the phone, Cate reflected that she was going to have a problem or two in that department as well.

As in, explaining to her next employer exactly why she'd been fired.

DANIEL SAID GOODBYE TO THE GUY feeding the pigeons—interesting fellow, as much of a bird geek as Cate—and turned to find her in the busy kaleidoscope of activity in the square. He spotted her on the waterfront side, holding a paper, and jogged over.

"Anything good in—" He stopped himself.

She looked as though someone had just told her the date of her death—and it was tomorrow.

"Cate? Are you all right?" Then he saw the cell phone in her hand. "Did you get bad news from home?" As far as he knew, her folks were alive and well in San Diego, but that didn't mean anything. These days, disaster struck without regard for health or preparation or merit. A person could get hit by a bus, or have their apartment broken into or have their car stolen. About the only things you could trust were love and history—and sometimes not even that.

"Yes," she said in a hollow voice.

"Your family? A friend?"

She held out the paper to him. "Page twenty-four."

What…? He flipped until he found the centerfold. His eyes widened as he took it in, and by the end of the photo essay, where he saw the credit, his jaw was hanging loose in shock.

"Dulcie did this?" was all he could think of to say. "But she shoots for *National Geographic*. She wouldn't waste her time on—" he checked the name of the rag "—*Entertainment News*. She'd be laughed off the free-lance roster."

Cate's jaw tightened and suddenly the angry woman of a week ago was back. "I'm glad to see your first thought is for *her* career."

He stared at her. "I didn't—"

"Because thanks to your fondness for the spotlight, I've just been informed by the university that I'm up for a disciplinary review."

"Why?" This wasn't computing. What did Vandenberg have to do with photos in a trashy paper? Why weren't the two of them laughing about this and ordering mimosas? Granted, the banana was a little extreme, and he could see a woman being upset about it, but it was nothing worse than the things he'd had to put up with.

She rolled her eyes. "Use your imagination, Daniel. The dean of humanities thinks I'm lowering the tone of the department. That my moral rectitude is in question. In short, I'm very likely going to be fired."

"Because of this?" He held the paper out and she snatched it away. "What business is it of theirs what you do? You're not representing the university here. You're on vacation. And we won't even go into the invasion of privacy and how many lawsuits I'm going to file. What you do with bananas in your own bedroom is your business."

"Apparently that's irrelevant. What is relevant is that it's now public. Let's deal with reality, not with how things should be." With jerky movements, she snapped the paper and folded it into sections. "I didn't realize that this is the price of getting involved with you. I knew I would have to make some compromises, but I never dreamed it would mean losing my career."

Now who wasn't dealing with reality? "Cate, you won't lose your career. Hell, I'm in the tabs all the time and mine just keeps getting better."

"Yes, well, fortunately you don't have to labor under the double standard. Women in academia can't behave the way men do, and that's that. The very first time I'm exposed to it, I lose everything. And isn't that nice and fair?"

"There must be something you can do."

"Of course. I'll go to the review, state my case, and watch them hand me my termination papers. Then I'll go home, have a glass of wine, and figure out whether I'd be happier making lattes at the coffee bar, or selling dresses at my favorite department store."

Her voice was shaking, but her shoulders were stiff, and when he reached for her, she turned to put the paper in her handbag and his fingers didn't make contact.

"Cate. Please."

"I'm sorry, Daniel." When she looked up, her eyes were full of tears. "I thought I could do this, but now I see I can't. I can't spend the rest of my life looking over my shoulder to see when the consequences of your actions are going to sneak up and bite me. I can't watch you in the spotlight while I stand in the dark, wondering what happened to the work I loved."

"You won't," he protested. What was happening here? This sounded like a breakup speech. "You won't lose your work. So what if a bunch of humorless prudes run you off? You have a terrific reputation as a scholar, Cate. You could get a job at any university in the country."

"Reputation. That's what it boils down to, doesn't it? Because of you I've just traded my reputation as a scholar for a reputation as an exhibitionistic tramp. Who likes bananas."

"Now you sound like a prude."

Wrong thing to say. Those dangerous slashes of color flared on her cheekbones. "Don't you attack me. I've had all I'm going to take. Thank you for the nice parts of this week. The sex was great. But I'm catching the first flight I can get back to New York and I don't want to see you ever again."

"Cate, you're overreacting. We can work this out together. Support each other. Cate, wait!"

But she didn't hear him. She was already halfway across the square, and the mocking cries of the gulls drowned out his voice.

_18_

IN A STROKE OF LUCK that seemed almost a miracle, Cate was able to get a standby seat on a nonstop flight to La-Guardia. By the time she and Daniel would have been getting around to dinner in California, she was flagging down a cab and speeding home to refuge in Queens.

She'd half expected a flock of catcalling reporters to be clustered around the door of her apartment building, but there was nothing but a few brown sparrows and the relative quiet of the evening. She let herself in, dropped her bag on the hardwood floor, and leaned against the door just breathing in the scent of furniture polish and books and the faint floral of the perfume she'd left at home.

Home.

She pushed herself away from the door and went into her bedroom, where she changed into pajamas, fell into bed and slept for twelve hours. When she woke the next day, there didn't seem to be a compelling reason to get up, and since she wasn't due into the office until tomorrow, she pulled the covers over her head.

In the late afternoon, her back was beginning to ache from being horizontal so much. She stumbled out into the kitchen and put on a pot of coffee. The mail hadn't piled up much, since she'd only been gone a few days, and there was nothing very interesting in it anyway except the new issue of the *American Journal of Archaeology*.

Maybe there'd be something interesting on TV. Something to take her mind out of this little maze of dread in which her brain was running this way and that like a trapped mouse. Because it was more than what faced her tomorrow during the staff meeting and the disciplinary review. It was more than meeting the eyes of her male colleagues and knowing they were thinking about that banana and what had been blurred out in the pictures.

Those things would fade, given enough time. What wasn't going to fade was this ache in her heart and this unquenchable need deep inside. Because her body didn't seem to realize she was never going to see Daniel again. It was ready for him now—and had been ever since she'd gotten on the plane. Every time a random image of him popped into her brain—leaning over her on the sand that first night, pulling her clothes off, feeding her bits of his steak—she again felt that tug of desire, that spurt of longing that she had experienced when he'd done those things. It was like her whole being was set on instant replay, and the constant ache of unfulfilled desire was driving her crazy.

Curling up in the corner of the couch with a pillow, she aimed the remote at the TV. Maybe she could find an action film with lots of explosions. Or even the news. Plenty of explosions there.

Gaaahh. You're starting to sound just like Daniel.

Making jokes about everything—especially when it's not appropriate.

Good. She'd latch on to all the bad things he did and maybe it would take her mind off what his hands could do to her, or the expression in his fathomless dark eyes when he looked at her, or—

"—like to welcome our next guest, archaeologist Dr. Daniel Burke!"

Cate's shoulders drooped and she gave up. Of course. It was Wednesday night. All of Stacy Mills's careful efforts to get Daniel into the Oakland TV studio on time had evidently paid off.

Common sense told Cate to flick the remote one more time and go find that action movie. But for some reason, her fingers wouldn't listen to common sense. Instead, they hit the record button and TiVo began to do its job. Not that she'd ever watch the program again once she'd recorded it. But she'd keep it around as sort of a modern cautionary tale and label it Here Be Dragons.

"Dr. Burke is with us on the third leg of a cross-country tour for his new book, *Lost Treasures of the World*," the attractive, redheaded program host told the cameras.

Cate figured the odds of the woman going back to the hotel with Daniel after the show were two to one. After all, he'd had his day of mourning.

"Tell me, Dr. Burke, what does it feel like to have earned this kind of recognition for your work?"

Daniel, Cate saw, looked as if he hadn't slept. Poor baby.

"I want to clarify that it isn't all my work," Daniel

said. "I lead highly qualified field teams who add to our knowledge every day. I'm just the front man, the logistics guy who pulls these things together. Giving me credit for our discoveries is like giving you credit for a successful show when you're surrounded by the production people who make it happen."

"That's very modest and very true, Dr. Burke. I'd like to take this opportunity to thank our studio production team." Her brilliant smile panned from one side of the screen to the other, and then she turned back to Daniel. "But what about Daniel Burke the private individual? We're familiar with your work in the field, but not many know who you really are underneath."

"There's a good reason for that, as you can imagine." The audience laughed.

"It's natural for a celebrity to want to keep his private life out of the spotlight," the woman agreed.

"That's just it," Daniel said. "I'm not a celebrity. I'm an archaeologist who made some discoveries and wrote—er, published a book. If I could keep people focused on the work of preserving antiquities, that's all I'd ask."

"But let's face it, Dr. Burke, for most people—if I may say so—a dashing adventurer who happens to be single and handsome is a more interesting subject than the preservation of antiquities. Wouldn't you agree?"

Daniel's face clouded and his dark eyes looked dangerous. Cate could see it was a struggle for him to remember he was on live television and his instinctive response wasn't going to be edited out later.

"I realize our culture has come to expect that if you're

in the public eye, you forfeit your privacy. But I've learned lately that the price for that is too high."

"What do you mean?" The interviewer leaned forward, exposing impressive and no doubt custom-designed cleavage.

"I suppose you've seen this week's issue of *Entertainment News?*"

The interviewer's smile was tight and she straightened. "You don't strike me as the type to read that kind of publication, Dr. Burke."

He shrugged. "On page twenty-four there's an article about me and an unnamed woman. That woman was very important to me, and because of the article she's no longer in my life."

The redhead looked shocked and put a hand to her chest, drawing the camera's close-up back to the cleavage. Cate sighed and wondered what would come out of Daniel's mouth next. A public declaration of undying love? That would rake in the headlines for sure. Everyone loved a tale of woe and loss.

Except, she had no doubt, the dean of humanities at Vandenberg University. And playing this recording for him probably wouldn't earn her any brownie points.

"Dr. Burke, that's terrible!" the interviewer said in shocked tones. "Are you going to file a lawsuit against the publication?"

"It's under consideration," Daniel said smoothly. "I'm an American with a reasonable expectation of privacy, which has been grossly invaded. However, if I receive a printed apology from the *Entertainment News* and in particular the photographer, who seems to have climbed up on a roof in order to shoot pictures of me and my companion in our bedroom, I'll drop consideration of a suit."

"On a roof! To shoot into a bedroom? Good heavens. Who's the photographer?"

Cate couldn't tell if the interviewer was faking her disapproval or not, but that was beside the point. *Entertainment News* was going to rake in the bucks on this week's issue, and that would probably soothe the sting of the printed apology by quite a bit.

"A woman named Dulcie Cavanaugh, who used to shoot for *National Geographic* but seems to have come down in the world."

Ooh, preemptive counterstrike! And on national television, too. If Ms. Cavanaugh thought she was ever going to get a serious job again, Cate speculated, she had another think coming.

"Dr. Burke, this is quite a commentary on the lengths the paparazzi will go to get a story. So, on a less emotional note, what is your next project?"

"I'll be going to Asia Minor for the summer," he said. "There's a site in the mountains east of the traditional site of Troy that looks very promising."

"Do you expect to find treasure?" she asked eagerly.

His smile was flat and lacked the seductive sparkle Cate remembered from his *Jah-Redd Jones* interview. "No," he said. "I've given up that expectation. The problem with treasure, I've discovered, is that it's all too easy for someone to take it away."

LATTE IN HAND, CATE MADE IT into her office undetected the next day, probably because it was only seven in the morning. Even Anne, who said she got more work done before the faculty came in than any other time of the day, wasn't in yet.

Cate needed the next half hour to regroup and find her courage. In the center of her blotter was the stack of message slips, with a couple of new ones added. Morgan Shaw had called again. Julia Covington wondered when Cate would be getting back. The dean's administrator advised that disciplinary review was scheduled for two o'clock, right before the staff meeting. Cate had a feeling she wouldn't need to bother with the latter.

After two o'clock, she'd no longer be on the staff.

The outer door opened and Anne came in. She'd shrugged off her sweater and put her briefcase away before she noticed that Cate's door was open and there was a body in the chair.

"Cate! What are you doing here so early? I'm so glad you're back. It feels like weeks since you were here."

Cate smiled ruefully. "I feel I've lived a whole lifetime, as a matter of fact." She held out the box containing the necklace, which she'd wrapped in fuchsia-pink tissue. "This is for you, from sunny California."

Anne ripped it open with the eagerness of a child at Christmas, and held up the sparkling bauble. "It's lovely! It looks just like that candy we used to get when I was a child." She put it on, and the necklace gave a jaunty air to her plain blouse. "I might need to update the look to match it, though. Maybe you can give me some fashion tips."

"We'll go shopping. After today, I'll probably have tons of time on my hands."

Anne wilted against the doorjamb, fingering the necklace as though it were made of worry beads. "I have to tell you, it's not looking good."

Cate tried to prepare herself for the worst. "Tell me."

"Well, you know how part of my job is to keep my ear to the ground and my mouth shut."

"And you do it well."

"So I was in the faculty break room and I heard a small crowd of the lecturers talking. Speculating."

"About what? Laying odds on how long I'll last?"

"No. Worse. About your love life. About—about the banana. And other things." Anne clasped her hands nervously. "Cate, I think you should sue that paper, too. I don't know if photos can be construed as libel, but it certainly is damaging to your career."

"I think you mean slander. And it isn't slander if it's true. Unfortunately, Daniel really did feed me a banana." She paused. "And I enjoyed it. Maybe you should pass that on to the lecturers. I might get a date out of the deal."

"Cate, I'm serious."

"So am I. So let's back up a little. What do you mean, I should sue, too? Who else is suing?"

"Well, Dr. Burke, of course. I saw him last night on TV."

Of course she had. Anne was a huge fan of Daniel's—the principal reason why Cate had been able to follow his career on the quiet, as it were. And the skunk had never gotten around to signing a copy of his wretched book for her.

"I can't believe he said that about you on national

TV. That you were important to him. Is that really true, Cate?"

"I'm sure it is." For all the good it did her.

"So you two got together at the conference? And then this photographer spoiled everything?"

"In a nutshell, yes."

"Well, Cate, my God, you're not going to let that come between you, are you? He said you were no longer in his life. What happened?"

If anyone but Anne had asked her that, she would have told them to mind their own business. But this was Anne, who had taken her home to her apartment on 9/11 because she couldn't get back to Queens. Who had stood by her during the department war last spring. Who had made endless cups of tea after classes were over and given her wise advice when Cate had needed it.

She couldn't blow Anne off. She was her friend and friends deserved the truth.

"It wasn't him, it was me," she said at last. "I know that sounds like a cliché, but in this case it's the truth. He wanted something long-term, but when this thing came out in the paper, I realized exactly what it could mean." She indicated the building with a vague movement of her hands. "And I was right. I'm going to lose my job because I fell in love with Daniel Burke."

She stopped, shocked she had actually said the words aloud.

"What was that?" Anne's gaze held amazement and humor. "Did I hear you say what I thought you said?"

"No." Cate shook her head as though a mosquito

were flying around it. "It's pointless to even think about him. God, forget I said that."

"I can," Anne told her. "But I'm not sure you can."

With her usual acuity, Anne had hit the nail on the head. Cate was never going to be able to forget. Hell, she'd carried a torch for Daniel for eight years without even knowing it, after only a few kisses. What did she have to look forward to now—another eight years of holding men up to Daniel's standard and finding they always came up short?

That was, if she planned to find someone else. At the moment it didn't feel very likely. Not with this ache in her heart and the tears so close to the surface that a word could trigger them. Not with the need so deep inside her that simply hearing his voice on the TV program was enough to give her erotic dreams.

"I have to," she said to Anne now. "I told him I couldn't live his life—always in the spotlight, always wondering if the next newspaper item is the one that will turn public opinion upside down and cause something else to be taken away from me. The media flurry and all that babble about how young I was when I came to Vandenberg was enough."

"Since when have you cared about public opinion? Not that I'd dream of reminding you that that media babble resulted in a very nice grant."

Cate glanced at her. "How would you like the lecturers speculating about your fondness for bananas? Or wondering how big your boobs really are?"

"Point taken." Anne sighed. "Well, if you want to go

out for dinner after work, let me know. You know I'm available if you need to talk this out."

Cate got up and hugged her. "You are the best friend a person could have. Let's see what happens at two o'clock and go from there."

Anne began to close Cate's door, then leaned in. "Don't forget to return your calls."

"I won't."

Somehow, between e-mail and returning most of the calls and going through the post, the morning disappeared. Anne brought her chicken soup for lunch, saying, "Because you'll need the strength."

And then it was two o'clock.

Outside the dean's private conference room, Cate took a deep breath, straightened her suit jacket, turned the handle and went in. At the conference table sat the dean of humanities, Roger Pathak, and her department head, Wilson Trowbridge. She supposed she should be grateful they hadn't called in the head of academics and the president of the institution. On the table in front of each man were a pad of paper and a copy of the *Entertainment News,* and her personnel folder sat next to the dean's elbow.

"Sit down, Dr. Wells."

She sat on the other side of the table, wishing she had a pad of paper, too. Then maybe she'd feel less like a child being called up on the carpet and more like a mature professional armed with a good argument.

"Dr. Wells, we've called this meeting to discuss the consequences of the article in this paper—" he glanced at it "—the *Entertainment News.* Are you familiar with the contents of it?"

"Yes." Along with half the nation.

"Do you have an explanation?"

"For what, sir?" The pictures? The paper? The fact that the only reason she was here was that the faculty couldn't resist the urge to gossip?

"I would think that would be obvious. But for the record, I'll spell it out. For the fact that you are in several of these pictures in—shall we say—very compromising positions."

"Sir, I believe our focus should be on bringing the paper to accept the consequences of invading my privacy. I was in my capacity as a private citizen at that time, not representing the university, and what I do with or without bananas in the privacy of my own bedroom is my business and no one else's."

"Dr. Wells, are you aware of what is being said about you on this campus?" Dr. Pathak demanded.

"No."

"I won't go into the salacious details, but there is a firestorm of speculation about—about—well, suffice to say that your character is being called into question not only among the faculty but among the students. And, consequently, their parents who pay their tuition."

"What, doesn't anyone else have a love life? Why is mine so interesting?"

"Everyone else keeps theirs in their own room," Dr. Trowbridge pointed out.

"Mine was in my own room, too. It wasn't my fault that Dulcie Cavanaugh and her big telephoto lens joined us."

"The fact remains that you are a laughingstock," Dr. Pathak said. Like this was her fault? Like she'd chosen this? "We can't allow our parents and benefactors to believe that our faculty routinely have themselves plastered all over the tabloids and then come back to class to teach their children."

"Oh, come on, sir," Cate said, goaded past endurance. "You can't tell me you're going to bring some kind of moral component into this. Not in this day and age. Not in New York."

"This school has a reputation that has stood for 120 years," he informed her. "If students deride the school, parents will join them. And benefactors. And funding sources. We can't allow that."

"What are you going to do?"

"We very much regret the necessity to consider such alternatives as these. We discounted suspension and termination immediately, of course."

Thank God for that. For the first time since she'd seen the wretched article, Cate felt the Gordian knot of tension under her rib cage ease a little. She wasn't going to lose her job. She could handle a lot if that was no longer hanging over her head.

Dr. Pathak opened her personnel file thoughtfully. Even from across the table and upside down, Cate could see the title of the document lying on top.

Application for Tenure.

Oh, my God. No.

"Your tenure package recently went to the committee for review, I understand."

"Two months ago," Cate whispered. It was a beautiful tenure package, too, with her publications, conference invitations and awards in all their shining glory. Eight years of doing the right things, talking up the right people and writing for the right journals was going to pay off in one of the coveted tenured positions at Vandenberg.

"I'm very much afraid, Dr. Wells, that the tenure committee has turned down your application," Dr. Pathak said. "I'm very sorry."

"Turned it down?" How could they do that? It was a perfect package. She had been the perfect candidate, and had just attained the perfect promotion to associate professor before they'd lured her over here with promises of early tenure. There was no way they could have turned it down. "I don't understand."

"I'm afraid that when push came to shove, this unfortunate business biased them in favor of Dr. Dileone, who was also competing for this position. You would have been my choice, of course, but my opinion wasn't solicited."

She'd always thought his smile was fake and now was no exception. "Sir, with all due respect, this is insane. I've done nothing wrong. You should be supporting me and threatening lawsuits against the paper, not ruining my career!"

"We realize there is less culpability here than, say, a faculty member abusing a student, but the public reputation of the school must be upheld at all costs. Clearly the tenure committee felt rather strongly about it." He rose and held out a hand. "Personally, I regret the school had to act in this way. Hopefully it will all blow over in a day or two, and you can get on with administering your exams and preparing for next term."

It was on the tip of Cate's tongue to say, "There won't

be any next term because I quit!" but years of doing the right thing had taught her to think first, blurt later. So she swallowed the words and, instead, turned on her designer heel and walked out of the conference room.

Her next call would be to Columbia. Maybe they hadn't filled her position yet.

19

DANIEL WHEELED THE CAMARO into the driveway of his modest house in Long Beach. A touch on the remote control on the visor sent the garage door up, and he parked it next to his Jeep. On autopilot, he yanked his bag out of the back seat, riffled through the mail, found one lonely beer in the fridge and wandered into his postage-stamp-sized backyard.

This was intolerable.

All six hours of the drive down from Oakland had been filled with the memory of Cate. She might as well have been sitting in the passenger seat, for all the good it did him trying to forget about her. The truth was that it was impossible.

The part he didn't get was why the stupid article was such a problem. He couldn't imagine any university in the country getting its knickers in a knot over such a thing when it was obvious the two of them were the victims in the whole affair. For Pete's sake, who cared what the *Entertainment News* printed? They were the scum on the bottom of the journalistic pond, as anyone in a grocery checkout line could tell you.

Daniel took a long pull on his beer and regarded his

juniper hedge sourly. There had to be more to it than just the pictures. What was it she really objected to?

There was only one answer he could see. A relationship with him. Somewhere between eating steak in bed and picking up that paper, she'd got cold feet and changed her mind. The photos only made a nice, neat excuse to hide behind.

Maybe without them, he'd have had a few more hours with Cate. Maybe not. *What spectacular timing you have, Dulcie, as always.*

Dulcie.

He pulled his cell phone from the clip on his belt and dialed a number that had become familiar. It only rang twice.

"Cavanaugh."

"Is this the D. N. Cavanaugh who shoots for *Entertainment News?*"

There was a long pause. "Danny?" she said with gratifying caution. What, did she think he was busy rigging her Venice apartment with a pipe bomb?

"Dulcie. Darling. I hope they're paying you what you deserve."

"There's no need to be cranky."

"Oh, I'm not cranky. Just curious. After all, if you're going to ruin someone's life you might as well be paid handsomely for it."

She snorted. In the background, he heard some kind of machinery and a long blast of a horn. Was she at a shipyard? Not that he cared. In fact, a slow boat to China would be a great place for her, as far as he was concerned.

"Don't give me that," she said. "You're so used to

being front-page news that a little item in a two-bit tabloid isn't even going to show up on your radar."

"You're right, it isn't," he agreed. "But I'm curious about two things. One, why you did it, and two, how you got up on the roof of that hotel."

"Oh, that was easy. I just rented the room across the hall from you and went out the window."

"And the rose and the perfume?"

"I don't know anything about a rose. But the perfume was mine. Did you think of me when you had her in bed?"

So Cate had been right.

"No, but she thought of you when you went after her clothes. She says thank you for not tearing them to pieces. Everything was repaired the same day."

"Is she still with you?" Dulcie's tone was sharp.

"Was that your plan? To scare her off?"

"You don't need a skinny little no-name like her, Danny. We had something fabulous. Once in a lifetime."

"Which I seem to remember you walked away from. You just up and left and the next thing I know, you're on assignment in Antarctica. Nothing very fabulous going on from my end."

She laughed, that magical laugh that had captivated him for months. Now it just sounded tired and overused. "I didn't know you were so high-maintenance, sweetie. I'm not the kind to write love notes and hide them in your lunchbox, you know? I have a career. And I didn't go to Antarctica. I just let you think so."

"Think the *Geographic* will be interested in your stuff when they know you've been invading people's privacy for the tabs?"

"Like they'd know," she scoffed. "Besides, you're a public figure. And I knew you wouldn't mind helping me out. Things have been a little tight."

"I might be a public figure but my companion wasn't. Your lens in our bedroom was out of line, Dulcie. I'm thinking about suing you and the paper."

Silence. "You wouldn't."

"Sure I would."

"You couldn't care less about that stuff. Someone points a camera at you and your first instinct is to ask for a comb."

"Maybe, but hers isn't."

"Oh, come on. Don't tell me you're going all Sir Galahad on me. I did it for you. You're always telling me how much publicity helps your career. For a fringe benefit, I thought I'd help you lose the chick and remember how good we were together. And voilà, you did."

"The only thing I remember is how amazingly self-centered you are, Dulcie. The only pleasure I got in bed with you was from jerking off after you'd fallen asleep. We are not getting back together. And you will be hearing from my attorneys."

"How dare you! I—"

How fitting that the last word he heard out of her mouth before he killed the connection should be *I*. Daniel rammed the phone into its holster at his belt and finished off the beer. There were no more questions in his mind about their long, strange trip up the coast, except for the question of who had put the rose on their pillows. It had probably been Galina or Ana, who had been too shy to admit it. At least a rose wasn't malicious, the way Dulcie had been malicious. Cate had been right all along.

So if she's right about that, maybe she's right about what the article will do to her career. Maybe you're just a little too secure, a little too complacent to see things from her point of view. You told Dulcie she was self-centered, but haven't you been behaving as if this were all about you?

And it had cost him Cate, just as it had eight years ago. Then, she had run because he overwhelmed her sexually. Well, she'd definitely grown out of that problem—he'd been hard-pressed to keep up with her curiosity and eagerness to learn all there was to know about seduction.

But he had overwhelmed her with his life this time. His fame had caught up with her and wiped out her needs and expectations for her own life and career as surely as an earthquake could take out a seemingly solid cliff. He hadn't explained to her what it was like, hadn't made any effort to prepare her…and when she was reeling from the shock, what had he done? Told her to shrug it off, as though the damage to her position at Vandenberg were nothing to him.

Was that the behavior of a man who loved a woman? Had he been just as shallow and self-absorbed as Dulcie? Could he blame Cate for catching the first plane away from him?

No.

Well, there was only one thing to do. He glanced at his watch. Nearly six o'clock in New York. Chances were slim she'd still be in the office, but he had to try.

He got Vandenberg's number from Information, and was put through by a helpful automated computer directory.

"Department of Archaeology and Anthropology," said a female voice with a Boston accent. Definitely not a computer.

"This is Dr. Burke calling for Dr. Wells, please."

After a moment of silence during which he wondered if he should repeat himself, the woman said slowly, "Dr. Wells has gone for the day. This is Anne Walters, her assistant. Can I help you?"

Anne, for whom Cate had bought a necklace of glass beads. For whom he had not bothered to sign a book, though Cate had asked him to more than once.

He winced at yet more evidence of his own self-centered behavior. "Did you like your necklace?" he found himself saying instead of "No, thanks," and hanging up.

"Yes, I did, very much." Anne's tone lost none of its caution. Or maybe it was diffidence. "Thank you."

"Oh, I had nothing to do with it. We were at this little art fair on the waterfront and she was dithering between that and a painting of the Golden Gate Bridge. If she got you the necklace, she could enjoy it, too, when you wore it. It's hard to wear a painting unless you're doing performance art."

"Good advice." Her tone warmed a degree or two.

"So has she really gone home or are you covering for her?"

"Oh, no, she left after the—"

Anne stopped, and he remembered that Cate was to have gone before a bunch of stuffed shirts who had the gall to think they could discipline her for something that wasn't her fault.

"The disciplinary review was today, wasn't it?"

Her sigh was audible, even long distance. "Yes."

"What happened?"

"Dr. Burke, you must know that's confidential."

"Dr. Burke does. But I'm not Dr. Burke at the moment. I'm just Daniel, who has faced some unpleasant truths about himself lately. And who has finally realized what a mistake it was to let her get on that plane. That's the guy who's asking, not that ass Dr. Burke with his face plastered all over the TV and the tabloids with only one thought in his mind—getting the next grant."

He shook his head in disgust at himself and sank onto his couch.

"Well, in that case," the woman said, "I'm not Mrs. Walters, dignified departmental assistant in a brown tweed skirt and sensible shoes. I'm Cate's friend wearing a spun-sugar necklace, and between you and me and the lamppost, the review board denied her tenure this afternoon."

Daniel felt his body sag as the consequences of his effect on Cate's life came home to him with a vengeance.

"The nasty part is, they got her over here from Columbia with a promise of early tenure so she could continue her work on the goddess cults. Now I guess that's going to come to a screeching halt."

"What's she going to do?" A hundred options presented themselves to him, none of them good.

Anne hesitated. "I'm not sure. I don't think she was serious about selling dresses at Bloomie's, though."

"You don't think she's going to give up teaching?"

"I honestly don't know, Dr. Burke."

"Daniel."

"Daniel. But this is all over the campus and people are blogging about it already. I heard her on the phone with Columbia, but it didn't sound promising. I think she's backed into a corner, and you know what happens when people feel that way."

He did indeed. "Anne, we have to do something."

"Well, I should think—" She stopped herself.

A very circumspect lady, this Anne Walters. The perfect assistant. Daniel wondered if she'd like a job in Long Beach.

"Sorry," she said instead.

"Oh, no, you don't. Spill. What were you going to say?"

"She'll kill me."

"So will I, only I'm much more inventive. After all, I dig up gravesites for a living."

"She's devastated right now, Dr.—Daniel. It's killing her that she gave you up and lost her career anyway. She—she loves you."

Daniel had heard the expression *my heart leaped* and had always rolled his eyes at the hyperbole. Except that his own heart had just—well, if it wasn't a leap, then it was at least a kick. As if it had just got a big shot of adrenaline, enough to galvanize him into fight-or-flight mode.

What's it going to be? Are you going to fight for her? Or flee?

"Did she tell you that?" He could hardly believe it. She hadn't even told him. And God knew he'd given her plenty of opportunity.

"It kind of slipped out."

"In that case, it's even more important that I do something. What do you suggest?"

"How soon can you get here?" Anne asked.

"There's a red-eye out of LAX."

"Good. By the time you land, I'll have thought of what to do. She's not planning to come in tomorrow, but she has to be back Monday to proctor her exams as well as Dr. Dileone's. So you'll have three days."

"I'm going to owe you, Anne. Big time."

"I know," she said. "I want an autographed copy of your book."

"If, between you and me, we can convince Cate that I love her, I'll dedicate the next one to you."

"That'll do for a start," she said.

20

HANDS ON HIPS, CATE TIPPED her head back and regarded the solid familiarity of her therapy cliff in upstate New York. Her car was parked half a mile away, at the trailhead, and there was no sound but her breathing, the calls of crows and sparrows, and the sighing of the wind in the trees. It was cloudy and there would probably be some rain later, but she figured there was enough time to climb to the ledge about sixty feet up, where the diffused light would probably have warmed the stone, and have a good long cry.

Anne had had to work late last night so she hadn't had the relief of being able to talk it out over curry and strong tea. And this morning, she should have gone in to meet with Dennis Dileone, give him her condolences on his wife's loss of her father, and prepare to proctor his exams as well as her own while he was out on bereavement leave.

But instead, she was taking a little informal bereavement leave for herself. A person should acknowledge the loss of a career and a relationship all in the same week. So if she wanted to climb a cliff and sit up there and cry, who was going to stop her?

The first ten feet were easy and didn't even require equipment. For the rest, she tightened her safety harness and set her cams in familiar cracks with swift efficiency, and within a few minutes of her personal record. She settled onto the ledge, pulled off her helmet, and let the pure sound of unobstructed wind blow through her. Below, the tops of the trees, fully leafed out now in early summer, made a fluffy, waving carpet, screening her from the worries and concerns of the world below.

Except that her own worries and concerns had packed themselves up here with her, locked in her head and in her heart.

Daniel.

Something inside her broke and tears pooled in her eyes, then flowed over. The wind felt cool on her face as it dried the tears and more came to replace them. She leaned back against the ancient granite and cried—for love, for loss and for discoveries she'd made about herself that she'd now be able to share with no one.

The digitized notes of the opening bars of the William Tell overture shrilled suddenly in the windy silence, and for a couple of seconds, as she snuffled and wiped the moisture from her cheeks, Cate could not place the sound.

Her cell phone.

She'd brought it in case of emergency, but not many people had this number. Her folks. Anne, Julia Covington and Dr. Trowbridge. All told, she wasn't in the best shape to talk to any of the above.

On the other hand, what if it was an emergency? Or what if Dr. Trowbridge had convinced the tenure committee to overturn their decision?

"Catherine Wells."

"Dr. Wells, I'm so glad I was able to reach you. This is Andrew Hoogbeck."

She sat on the ledge, her feet swinging in the air, and tried to get her mouth working.

"Dr. Hoogbeck, what—what a surprise."

"I hope I'm not interrupting your work."

"No, I'm, er, a bit up in the air at the moment. How are you?"

"I'm very well, thank you. I've been at the fossil site practically twenty-four hours a day since the plesiosaur was discovered. It's been very exciting."

"I'm glad, but Dr. Hoogbeck, I'm afraid I'm at a loss. First, I'm curious as to how you got this number, and second, I'm wondering how I can possibly help you."

"Both very legitimate questions, and happily both easy to answer. Forgive me for not explaining first. My mind has been so consumed with securing the site and making arrangements that I'm losing touch with my social graces. Dr. Burke gave me your number."

Dr. Burke did not have her number. She'd never gotten around to giving it to him. He would not have called her parents, so he must have called the school. She was going to throttle Anne Walters with her pink candy necklace.

"As for the second question," Dr. Hoogbeck went on, "it's not what you can do for me, but what I am in a position to do for you."

"For me?" Cate looked down between her feet and for the first time wished she were on the ground. She felt a sudden need to pace and throw things.

"Dr. Burke informs me that your position at Vandenberg University is, shall we say, not what you were led to believe when you took the job there."

"With all due respect, sir, Dr. Burke had no right to tell you any such thing." Cate snatched a rock the size of her fist off the ledge and lobbed it straight out into space. As it crashed into the canopy, a flock of startled birds leaped into the air, screeching.

If she could have screeched, too, she would have.

"I understand your feelings, Dr. Wells. But I have a proposition for you."

Oh, surely not. The dignified and verbose Dr. Hoogbeck could not possibly have read the *Entertainment News.* If he said one word about bananas, this phone was going to follow the rock into the treetops, and she'd apologize to the birds later.

He seemed to take her outraged silence as an invitation to continue. "The processing of the plesiosaur is going to take years, Dr. Wells, including its transportation from Big Sur to the Museum of Natural History in Santa Fe, New Mexico, where I have just been offered a position."

"Congratulations, sir." What on earth did this have to do with her? What had Daniel told him that would make him think she cared two hoots about fossils?

"Thank you. I'm very pleased about it, myself. But it brings me to the problem of the position I will leave empty at UNM Los Brazos."

Mystery solved. He was calling her for a recommendation. But why? "Dr. Hoogbeck, I'm afraid I don't know any paleogeologists' work well enough to recommend anyone to you. It's a couple of million years out of my bailiwick."

He laughed comfortably. "You misunderstand me, my friend. Are you familiar with the position I currently hold?"

She knew she should have read that conference brochure more carefully. "Ah—"

"I'm the dean of the School of Natural History and Science at UNMLB. A rather cumbersome title for a very rewarding job—but my plesiosaur is going to make it impossible for me to continue there. I would like to know if you would like to come out and talk with the board of regents about taking the position."

Cate's whole face went slack and she forgot how to speak. Below her, the birds settled back into the trees while she held the cell phone to her ear and tried to form a coherent reply.

"Dean? Me?" she finally managed to say.

"Indeed, yes. I can't think of anyone more qualified than yourself. Of course, it's a state school and not a private one, so you'd be surrounded with less luxury than you're no doubt used to, but northern New Mexico is a beautiful place. And the opportunities for study far outweigh its more spartan working conditions."

"Yes, I know." Northern New Mexico was full of deep blue skies and red sandstone cliffs and endless vistas of space. Mountains and mesas instead of skyscrapers and traffic. Hawks instead of airplanes. The sound of the wind instead of the honking of irritated cabbies. And through it all, that sense of being rooted in ancient history and traditions and spirit. There was a reason the tourist board called it the Land of Enchantment. "But—"

"And it wouldn't be a lonely place by any means. One or two of the archaeologists you met at the conference are based in Albuquerque. And your colleague Dr. Burke would be close by."

"What?" Lucky thing her equipment was still in place or she might have pitched over the edge in sheer astonishment.

"I understand a federal think tank for the preservation of domestic antiquities has been pursuing him for quite some time. They're based in Los Brazos as well. His media contacts will be invaluable in such a job, I would think."

"Yes," she agreed faintly. This was all too much. How had it all come about? Was the atmosphere up here thinner than she'd thought? Could she be hallucinating the whole thing?

"I'm sure you'll want to give this careful consideration, do your research and whatnot," Dr. Hoogbeck told her, "but I hope in the end that I'll see you in New Mexico. Do you think a week will be enough time?"

It would take her a week to recover from the shock of all of this. And to decide whether she wanted to be within five states of Daniel Burke when all was said and done. "Yes. Thank you, Dr. Hoogbeck. I'll call you in a week."

He signed off with happy noises, among which she detected the words *delighted* and *plesiosaur*. Shaking her head, she tucked the phone back in its zippered pocket, checked her pins and began to rappel back down the cliff. Behind her, in the windy silence, she heard the crunch of gravel on the rocky trail, which meant someone was coming and it was time to go in any case. Somehow, when she was forced to share her therapy wall, it never had the same benefits as when she was alone.

She bounced gently down the last ten feet and touched ground again. She could hear clearly the sound of a pair of booted feet on the trail, and she coiled her lines quickly and unbuckled her harness. The carabiners clanged as she dropped them into their pocket in her backpack.

The footsteps stopped at the edge of the clearing and she turned to greet the climber—he had to be a climber, not a hiker, because the trail pretty much terminated here.

"Did you know there are three different kinds of hawks up here?" Daniel Burke said and smiled at her as though the past few days had never happened.

"FOUR, ACTUALLY," she corrected him, then closed her eyes briefly as if she were giving herself a mental slap at being tricked into speaking.

Daniel's hopes of a rapturous reunion, which had been more of a dream than an actual hope, wavered and then recovered. He hadn't come all the way across the country and driven four hours into the wilderness to be put off now. No way. He'd say his bit and if that still didn't work, then at least he'd know inside that he'd done his best.

It was all up to Cate now.

"How are you?" he asked. It was a legitimate question—she looked like one of his students had on the brink of a cliff before someone had let Daniel know the kid was terrified of heights. But Cate had no such fears.

A closer look revealed that her eyes were reddened with the wind and he could swear she'd had about as much sleep in the last twenty-four as he had. Which was next to none.

She didn't bother to answer his question, legitimate or not. "What are you doing here?"

"I came to find you."

Her jaw tightened in a way that was becoming distressingly familiar. "Anne had no right to tell you where I was."

"She didn't." Not really. "You hadn't said where you were going, so we figured out a couple of the most likely places. This was one of them."

She brushed past him and slung her pack over her shoulder. He hoisted his own—which contained not much more than a bottle of water and a *Pocket Guide to North American Birds* that he'd picked up in the airport in Denver—and followed her.

"Aren't you even a little glad to see me?" he asked as she marched ahead of him. Her booted feet were sure on the path, as though she'd walked it many times. According to Anne, she had. This was the place she came when the pressure got to be too much. Daniel regretted the part he'd played in adding to that burden.

"Why should I be?" she replied without bothering to turn her head. "Because of you, I lost something I really valued."

"I heard."

That stopped her. "I suppose Anne told you that, too."

"Yes."

"I swear, I am going to murder that woman. How dare she tell you confidential things about my life. My career is none of your business—or hers, either!"

She took off so fast it took him twenty feet to catch

up. "She dares because I told her I loved you. She cares about you, so she told me everything I needed to know in order to find you."

They had reached the parking lot in record time. He had parked his rental car next to her modest little sedan. After tossing her pack into the trunk, she slammed it and snapped, "How nice. You tell her but you don't tell me. Not that it matters."

"Cate." He took her by both arms and held her the way a person might hold an injured wild bird so that it won't hurt itself anymore. "I told you when we were in California. And it's still true. I came here to say how sorry I am that my past ruined your career at Vandenberg. Andy Hoogbeck told me when I discovered his plesiosaur that if he could ever do anything for me, I was to call him. So when I was waiting for my connection in Denver, I did."

The angry color was fading from her cheeks, but her eyes were still red, as though she were on the point of tears.

"Were you looking for a job?" she asked.

"Not for myself. The folks at this think tank in New Mexico have been after me for at least a year about taking a directorship and becoming a spokesman for the government about land use and preservation."

"Dr. Hoogbeck told me."

Hope bloomed inside him. "So he called you already about the vacant position. And?"

"I have a week to think about it."

It was now or never. Either she wanted to be with him or she didn't, but Daniel would never know unless he stepped out, like Indiana Jones, into the air over the chasm of distrust and discovered for himself whether there was anything there to walk on.

"I've had a few days to think, Cate, and hold up a mirror to myself to see the guy I really am. And the truth is, I'm not so happy about that guy. I figure it's time to take control of the media with this new job, and do some good with it instead of using it to get the next grant for my own research." He took a breath. "After the expedition in Turkey, I'm definitely moving to New Mexico. And I would love it if you chose that path, too. It's completely up to you, but I wanted you to know how I felt."

"It's…a very tempting offer," she said slowly.

"It's a great school, with all kinds of excavation possibilities right in your backyard. And you'll make a terrific dean."

"I didn't mean the job." She looked up and at last her gaze met his. "I meant you."

"I'm glad I still tempt you," he said softly. "For the last couple of days I was sure you hated me."

"I did," she said with all the bone-scraping honesty he loved in her. "But what I hate even more is not being in control of my future. Of fearing other people more than having confidence in myself. Of making academics more important than love. That's a terrifying quality in a person."

"And now?"

"Do you remember that scene in *The Last Crusade* where Indy steps into the air over that sheer drop?"

Great minds really did think alike. "That was me, a minute ago."

She moved into his arms with a suddenness that surprised him…but his body knew what to do. He hugged her fiercely.

"And this is me, now. I'm going to do it, Daniel."

"You're going to head for the desert? The Land of Enchantment?" Better check, just in case she was talking about something else.

"I wouldn't want you out there all by yourself. You might fall off a cliff. Or mistake a shark's tooth for a potsherd."

It was hard to form a proper kiss when you were grinning.

But Daniel managed it.

21

WHEN THE PHONE RANG SHORTLY after 8:00 a.m., Morgan Shaw was already in the antique shop, though she wouldn't flip over the Open sign for another two hours. The truth was, she was too jumpy to sleep. While Adam had lain sprawled on the sheets with his enviable ability to conk out no matter what the circumstances, she'd dressed, made coffee and, cup in hand, had headed over to the shop.

Dr. Wells might call at any time in response to her messages, and Morgan meant to be there when she did.

When the phone finally rang, even though she'd been expecting it for days, she still jumped as a *zing!* of adrenaline shot through her.

"Morgan Shaw."

"Ms. Shaw, this is Catherine Wells from Vandenberg University, returning your call." A pause. "Calls. Sorry about that. I just got back to the office this morning."

"No problem. I should probably apologize to your assistant for driving her crazy."

When the professor replied, Morgan could almost hear a smile. "She's got a pretty tough skin. So. I know you're very anxious to hear what I was able to discover about your carved box."

Morgan's heart rate picked up a little with anticipation. "Yes, I am." Understatement of the year. "I really don't know why I care so much."

"Probably for the same reason I care about images of the female under a thousand years of dirt and Da—other archaeologists care about bits of pottery and stone."

"It's nice to know I'm not alone in my lunacy. So… what did you find out?"

"I consulted with Dr. Daniel Burke, of whom you may have heard."

"The name rings a bell, but I don't know where from."

The professor chuckled, as if this were funny. "He's a well-known symbologist specializing in the ancient world. I believed the carvings would interest him, and I was right. They did."

"And?" Morgan's chest was feeling tight. Would she never get to the point?

"The carvings have similarities to Egyptian images, but he said they definitely weren't Egyptian. However, around 3000 BCE, Egypt expanded its borders pretty significantly, and a number of desert kingdoms were conquered. Their royalty, if they were still alive, were taken prisoner and their assets seized. The common people were assimilated into the Egyptian population. But before this happened, what we call *culture bleed* occurred."

"What's that?"

"Elements of Egyptian culture were adopted by the artist who carved the box before his culture was overrun. In this way we can date it pretty accurately and my expert postulates it was created in the El Gibi kingdom by someone from the educated class. Not royalty and not a laborer, but someone who would have had a number of years of schooling, especially in mathematics, and possibly some training in his chosen means of expression."

"Wow," Morgan breathed, taking notes in rapid shorthand. "Your expert is pretty good."

"Yes, he is." Another pause. "There's more."

"I'm all ears."

"He noticed something in the photos that you and I completely missed when we had the real thing in front of us. Some of the carvings on the top connect to form the shape of a star."

"A star?" Could that be where a key might fit? Morgan's thoughts flew to what the papers were calling the White Star amulet—the valuable ivory artifact that had been stolen from the Stanhope auction house in New York not long ago. "It wouldn't be about the size of a silver dollar and have five points, would it?"

After a moment, Dr. Wells said, "Yes, it would, as a matter of fact. Have you found out more about it?"

Morgan felt a little short of breath, and a strange, prickly feeling was tiptoeing down the back of her neck and across her shoulders. "I don't know if you've seen the papers around here—"

"No, I've been in California, and then I took a couple of days upstate—rock climbing in the same area where I met your sister."

"Right," Morgan said. "Well, an ivory amulet they're calling the White Star recently came to light and I guess there's been a regular treasure hunt over it. But Cate—"

she forgot formality in the excitement of the moment "—what if it's the key to this box?"

"That…seems highly unlikely." The other woman's voice sounded a little breathless, too.

"Not if you know about the book."

"Book? There's a book about it now? Why didn't you say so before?"

"Because I didn't know enough when I saw you." Morgan took a deep breath, willing her heart to slow down. "A couple of months ago I got a shipment of rare books, and among them was this French text that was practically crumbling apart. When Cass and I were looking through it, we saw a picture of a star amulet that was identical to the one stolen from the auction house."

"Coincidence. Or maybe there is more than one amulet floating around. It's a pretty common shape."

"It's possible," Morgan allowed, "but not in view of the legend."

"Okay, I'm listening," Cate said, her interest obviously caught.

"I'm planning a trip to France shortly, so I'm taking language lessons," Morgan went on. "For practice, I took a stab at translating the text around the illustration of the star. Turns out it's the story of two sisters, one of whom is the queen of this little kingdom, who marries her younger sister's true love because he's the most famous soldier in the land."

"Poor girl. The younger one, I mean."

"But before he marries her sister, the younger princess gives him a gift."

"Let me guess. The White Star."

"Right. I have it right here." Morgan had written out the legend, with her translation interspersed between the lines. *"La petite princesse a donné l'étoile blanche à son amour vrai. Mais elle n'a pas su qu'elle devait être la clef à un trésor précieux."*

"Okay, you're going to have to translate that one for me," Cate laughed. "I'm fluent in Greek and Latin but French defeats me."

"It says, 'The little princess gave the white star to her true love. But she did not know it was to be the key to a most precious treasure.'"

"What could that be? A jewel of some kind?"

"I doubt we'll ever know. The soldier gets killed in battle and the queen and her sister take what they can carry and flee into the desert."

"And then what?"

Morgan looked down at her translation. "I don't know. I haven't translated any more after that. Things seem to get a little fuzzy, historically speaking."

"So you think this ivory amulet is the key to a box you found in your shop at the same time as you discovered a French legend about it. Morgan, doesn't this all strike you as just too coincidental to be believed?"

Trust a scientist to be skeptical. But the woman had been an enormous help. Morgan could hardly blame her for not believing something that was, in its essence, pretty far-fetched.

"Maybe it is coincidence. But what if it isn't? What if it's fate bringing all three things—amulet, box and legend—together?"

"For what purpose?"

"I don't know. Maybe there's something in this box that's meant to be shared with the world. Maybe not. But what if it's all come full circle for some higher purpose? Like maybe I'm supposed to do something with it?"

"I guess you'll need to figure that out. But for now, my assistant tells me that I have an exam to supervise, so I'm going to wish you luck and say goodbye."

"Thanks for all your help, Cate. It was a lucky day that my sister got lost in the woods and ran into you."

"And because of that, you brought me the box and I was reunited with *my* true love. Maybe there's something in that legend after all."

Morgan knew she had to go, so she didn't press Cate for details. Instead, she wished her well and hung up.

She got up and fetched the box from the safe. Turning it over and over, she traced for the hundredth time the images carved into its surface. And for the first time, she ran a finger slowly over the top of the box, discovering the star shape where the amulet might fit.

Common sense urged her to be satisfied with what she knew and leave it at that. She had other things to think about—the health of her marriage being at the top of that list. And the trip to France.

But great adventures never began with common sense. True love was never won on logic.

Carefully, Morgan wrapped the box in soft shipping material and took it out to the car. She'd sacrifice a pair of shoes to give it room in her suitcase. When she and Adam got to France, she would find a way to put the magic back into their relationship. To restore that deep sense of all-consuming, eternal love she'd been craving practically all her life.

When she got to France, Morgan promised herself, she would find the key.

If you enjoyed what you just read,
then we've got an offer you can't resist!

Take 2 bestselling love stories FREE!

Plus get a FREE surprise gift!

Clip this page and mail it to Harlequin Reader Service®

IN U.S.A.	IN CANADA
3010 Walden Ave.	P.O. Box 609
P.O. Box 1867	Fort Erie, Ontario
Buffalo, N.Y. 14240-1867	L2A 5X3

YES! Please send me 2 free Harlequin® Blaze™ novels and my free surprise gift. After receiving them, if I don't wish to receive anymore, I can return the shipping statement marked cancel. If I don't cancel, I will receive 6 brand-new novels each month, before they're available in stores! In the U.S.A., bill me at the bargain price of $3.99 plus 25¢ shipping and handling per book and applicable sales tax, if any*. In Canada, bill me at the bargain price of $4.47 plus 25¢ shipping and handling per book and applicable taxes**. That's the complete price and a savings of at least 10% off the cover prices—what a great deal! I understand that accepting the 2 free books and gift places me under no obligation ever to buy any books. I can always return a shipment and cancel at any time. Even if I never buy another book from Harlequin, the 2 free books and gift are mine to keep forever.

151 HDN D7ZZ
351 HDN D72D

Name	(PLEASE PRINT)	
Address	Apt.#	
City	State/Prov.	Zip/Postal Code

Not valid to current Harlequin® Blaze™ subscribers.

Want to try two free books from another series?
Call 1-800-873-8635 or visit www.morefreebooks.com.

* Terms and prices subject to change without notice. Sales tax applicable in N.Y.
** Canadian residents will be charged applicable provincial taxes and GST.
All orders subject to approval. Offer limited to one per household.
* and ™ are registered trademarks owned and used by the trademark owner and/or its licensee.

BLZ05   ©2005 Harlequin Enterprises Limited.